P9-CFT-023

MONTICELLO PUBLIC LIBRARY
512 E. LAKE AVE.
MONTICELLO, WI 53570

CIVIL WAR

A to Z

A Confederate veteran and a Union veteran clasp hands at a gathering of former soldiers many years after the war.

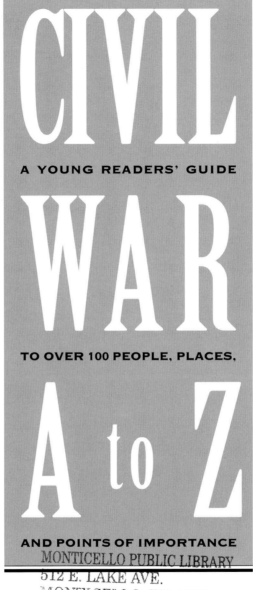

CIVIL WAR A to Z

A YOUNG READERS' GUIDE

TO OVER 100 PEOPLE, PLACES,

AND POINTS OF IMPORTANCE

MONTICELLO PUBLIC LIBRARY
512 E. LAKE AVE.
MONTICELLO, WI 53570

NORMAN BOLOTIN

DUTTON CHILDREN'S BOOKS   NEW YORK

Copyright © 2002 by Norman P. Bolotin/The History Bank

All rights reserved. No part of this publication may be reproduced or transmitted in any form or by any means, electronic or mechanical, including photocopy, recording, or any information storage and retrieval system now known or to be invented, without permission in writing from the publisher, except by a reviewer who wishes to quote brief passages in connection with a review written for inclusion in a magazine, newspaper, or broadcast.

Library of Congress Cataloging-in-Publication Data

Bolotin, Norm, 1951–
Civil War A to Z : a young readers' guide to over 100 people, places, and points of importance / Norman Bolotin.— 1st ed.
p. cm.
Includes bibliographical references.
Summary: Alphabetically arranged articles present over 100 people, places, and points of importance of the Civil War.
ISBN 0-525-46268-6
1. United States—History—Civil War, 1861–1865—Encyclopedias—Juvenile literature.
[1.United States—History—Civil War, 1861–1865—Encyclopedias.] I. Title.
E468.B73 2002
973.7'03—dc21   2001033370

Published in the United States by Dutton Children's Books
a division of Penguin Putnam Books for Young Readers
345 Hudson Street, New York, New York 10014
www.penguinputnam.com

Series development/book production: The History Bank, Woodinville, Washington
Editing, research, and development: Laura Fisher, Christine Laing
Design: Sandra Harner
Map design: Kelly Burch

Printed in China   First Edition   10 9 8 7 6 5 4 3 2

For CAL, for all she's done

&

For HLB, for all she has before her

MONTICELLO PUBLIC LIBRARY
512 E. LAKE AVE.
MONTICELLO, WI 53570

Author's Note

I cannot imagine a more intense time to have lived in the United States than during the Civil War. This was not a war between countries or strangers; it was a war between brothers and friends, fathers and sons.

The Civil War was about preserving very different ways of life in the North and the South. It was bloody and violent, and it grew far beyond what anyone had expected. Women from southern plantations and northern cities alike thought their husbands and fiancés would come home victorious—in a matter of weeks or perhaps months—and life would return to normal. Four agonizing years later, when the war finally ended, virtually every family in the nation had been touched—often devastated—by the war. The very fabric of the country's society, economy, and everyday life was torn to shreds.

In this book, and in the previous six volumes in our *Young Readers' History of the Civil War*, my goal was to share the personal stories, not just the facts and the figures and the important dates in history. There is no better way for a reader, a student of any age, to understand the Civil War than through the words of those who lived and died for what they believed and often for what they did not understand.

I hope that this quick A-to-Z reference will be used over and over again. It will be even more successful if it becomes the impetus for studying a battle more fully, for reading the New York or Atlanta newspapers from the war years, or for looking into biographies, diaries, letters, and other materials that bring this tumultuous time in our history to life.

Norm Bolotin
Woodinville, Washington

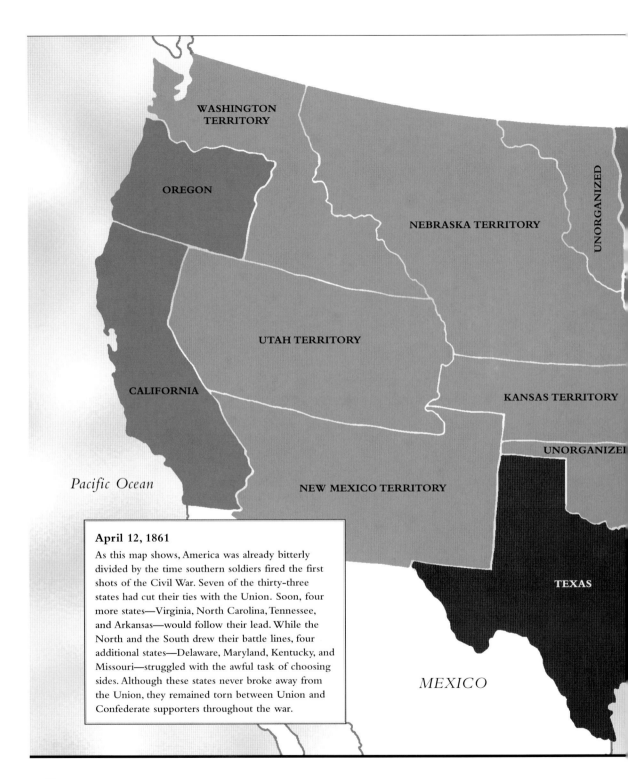

WASHINGTON TERRITORY

OREGON

NEBRASKA TERRITORY

UNORGANIZED

UTAH TERRITORY

CALIFORNIA

KANSAS TERRITORY

Pacific Ocean

UNORGANIZED

NEW MEXICO TERRITORY

TEXAS

April 12, 1861

As this map shows, America was already bitterly divided by the time southern soldiers fired the first shots of the Civil War. Seven of the thirty-three states had cut their ties with the Union. Soon, four more states—Virginia, North Carolina, Tennessee, and Arkansas—would follow their lead. While the North and the South drew their battle lines, four additional states—Delaware, Maryland, Kentucky, and Missouri—struggled with the awful task of choosing sides. Although these states never broke away from the Union, they remained torn between Union and Confederate supporters throughout the war.

MEXICO

CANADA

MINNESOTA

WISCONSIN

MICHIGAN

IOWA

ILLINOIS

INDIANA

OHIO

MISSOURI

KENTUCKY

MAINE

VERMONT

NEW HAMPSHIRE

MASSACHUSETTS

RHODE ISLAND

CONNECTICUT

NEW YORK

PENNSYLVANIA

NEW JERSEY

Washington, D.C.

DELAWARE

MARYLAND

WEST VIRGINIA★

VIRGINIA★

NORTH CAROLINA★

Atlantic Ocean

TENNESSEE★

ARKANSAS★

SOUTH CAROLINA

Charleston

Ft. Sumter

LOUISIANA

MISSISSIPPI

ALABAMA

GEORGIA

Gulf of Mexico

FLORIDA

Free States

Slave States

Confederate States
April 12, 1861

Territories

★Within a month after the first shots
were fired at Fort Sumter, these
states had joined the Confederacy.
West Virginia seceded from the
Confederacy and rejoined the Union
as a new state on June 20, 1863.

©2001 Norman P. Bolotin/The History Bank

⭐ ABOLITIONISTS

Those people, black and white, who wanted to end, or abolish, slavery in the United States, were known as abolitionists. The battle over slavery was as old as the country itself. The Constitution did not prohibit slavery, but abolitionists usually cited "higher" laws for their belief that slavery was a sin in the eyes of God, a crime against humanity.

Many abolitionists took strong action or spoke out about their cause: In 1831, Nat Turner led a bloody slave uprising in Virginia in which fifty-seven whites and eventually most of the slaves involved were killed; William Lloyd Garrison, publisher of *The Liberator*, spent nearly a half century writing against slavery; former slave Frederick Douglass and the American Anti-Slavery Society campaigned for the freedom of slaves; many abolitionists aided runaway slaves by participating in the Underground Railroad; and many more marched and protested vigorously for what they considered an issue of human rights.

The abolitionist movement not only caused conflicts over whether slavery should be abolished but was a major factor in bringing about the Civil War. The South, dependent on a plantation economy and the use of slaves, felt it had no choice but to go to war to protect its way of life. "Let us show at least as much spirit in defending our rights as the Abolitionists have evinced in denouncing them," said the eloquent senator from South Carolina John C. Calhoun. He was angrily rejecting the notion that the federal government had any right to tell individual states what they could or could not do with regard to slavery or any other issue.

Most Northerners—as well as the federal government and even President Lincoln—were not abolitionists but fought the Civil War to preserve the Union. Those who were against slavery on ideological grounds were not automatically abolitionists, although many labeled them as such.

★ ALCOTT, LOUISA MAY (1832–1888)

Louisa May Alcott

Louisa May Alcott started writing at an early age to earn money to help support her impoverished family. Her father, Bronson Alcott, was one of America's most influential educational reformers and took part in founding a communal farm, Fruitlands, which failed. In 1863, Alcott first gained recognition for *Hospital Sketches,* a book based on the letters she wrote while serving as a Civil War nurse in Washington, DC. During her lifetime she published more than thirty books, including the classic *Little Women,* a largely autobiographical novel about four sisters coming of age in New England during the Civil War. An active social reformer, Alcott fought for abolition, temperance, and women's rights. In 1879, she became the first woman in Concord, Massachusetts, to register to vote.

★ ANDERSON, ROBERT (1805–1871)

Although Kentuckian Robert Anderson was a former slaveholder and sympathetic to the South, he remained

Major Robert Anderson, shown here with his family, commanded Union troops at Fort Sumter. He was forced to surrender the fort to his own former student at the U.S. Military Academy, Confederate General P.G.T. Beauregard.

absolutely loyal to the Union. He knew that a civil war would destroy family, states, and the nation. In early 1861, Anderson was commanding a federal garrison at Fort Sumter, which defended the Charleston, South Carolina, harbor. Anderson was forced to return fire when the fort was bombarded by Confederate cannon early on the morning of April 12, 1861. The attack was led by General P.G.T. Beauregard, who had been a student of Anderson's at the U.S. Military Academy at West Point. Now they were exchanging the first shots of battle of the Civil War. Anderson had the difficult task of defending the Union fort against people legally his countrymen but who claimed the fort belonged to the new Confederate government. See *Fort Sumter*.

★ ANDERSONVILLE PRISON

No place epitomized the horrors of the Civil War more than Andersonville Prison, in Georgia. Andersonville was built as a 16.5-acre stockade; ten acres were added later. Initially planned to house ten thousand prisoners, just six months after it opened in 1864, three times that number were crowded inside. Each man had a space of less than six feet by six feet. There was little shelter or sanitation and

Andersonville was infamous for the death and disease that occurred there. Prisoners faced relentless, oppressive heat, insects, disease, and virtually no sanitation. Those without tents built their own huts out of anything they could find—twigs, pieces of wood, and any scrap left behind by dead prisoners. Virtually everyone was sick, and by the time the war ended, thirteen thousand prisoners had died at Andersonville.

only minimal food; the sweltering heat and disease eventually killed 13,000 of the 40,000 Union troops held there during the war. During the hottest weeks of summer, more than one hundred Union soldiers died at Andersonville every day. An estimated 30,000 of the nearly 200,000 Union troops in Confederate prisoner-of-war camps died during the war. It was not much better in the North, where 26,000 of the 214,000 Confederate prisoners died in captivity. See *Medical Care*.

The dead at Andersonville were buried in trenches, contributing to the diseases there, as well as the stench in the hot Georgia summers.

⭐ ANTIETAM, BATTLE OF (SHARPSBURG)

The Battle of Antietam, fought along Antietam Creek near the town of Sharpsburg, Maryland, was costly to both sides. After winning the second Battle of Bull Run, Confederate General Robert E. Lee moved his troops into Maryland, just forty miles from the nation's capital. He hoped to destroy important Union railroad lines in Pennsylvania and find much-needed clothes and supplies for his army. Union General George McClellan's Army of the Potomac met him near Sharpsburg, and for fourteen hours on September 17, 1862, a total of more than one hundred thousand

Bodies lie scattered on the battlefield after the bloodiest single day of the war. On September 17, 1862, Union and Confederate troops suffered twenty-three thousand casualties at Antietam.

men and five hundred cannon tore away at each other. When nightfall came, more than twenty thousand men were either dead or in the field hospitals that had been hastily set up in the nearby valleys and hills. The battle, in strict military terms, was a draw, with neither North nor South gaining an advantage. But the North considered it a victory because Union troops had stopped the Confederate Army in its first attempt at invading northern territory.

★ APPOMATTOX COURT HOUSE

The Civil War officially ended at Appomattox Court House in Virginia on April 9, 1865, when General Robert E. Lee surrendered his army to Union General Ulysses S. Grant. Other Confederate troops had not yet surrendered but would in the coming weeks as word of the official end of the war reached them. President Lincoln celebrated, as did thousands in Washington, DC. At the surrender, with Lincoln's approval, Grant gave southern troops much-needed food, and the surrendering soldiers were granted an immediate pardon, ensuring that none could be tried for treason for having fought against the Union. Lee asked that his troops be allowed to keep their horses, since they

General George Armstrong Custer will forever be known for leading his men to slaughter in Montana during the Indian Wars, but he was the officer receiving the surrender flag from Lee at Appomattox. N. Albert Sherman of the First Vermont witnessed the formal end of the war and wrote about it in a letter to his cousin.

General Custer sent [Lee] word that it must be "unconditional surrender." They drew up on a hill about one mile from Appomattox Court House. General Sheridan came up and he and General Lee went into the little house and General Grant was sent for as he was not far away. I went over to the rebel camp in the PM, and had a chat with our Southern brethren most of whom were glad of the doings of the day.

owned them before the war, and Grant agreed. The war was over, but the price was beyond calculation: More than six hundred thousand American soldiers had died.

★ ARMY OF NORTHERN VIRGINIA

The main army of the Confederacy was the Army of Northern Virginia, commanded by Robert E. Lee. Earlier called the Confederate Army of the Potomac, Lee renamed it to avoid confusion—since the North had its own Army of the Potomac. Lee was acknowledged as a great tactician, but his tactics often brought victory at a high cost in dead and wounded. Forty of the fifty units suffering the highest casualties for the South were in the Army of Northern Virginia. In 1862, at its largest and healthiest, the army numbered nearly one hundred thousand troops. Those numbers were severely depleted by the time Lee surrendered at Appomattox Court House in April 1865.

General Lee signs the surrender papers while Grant (seated) and other Union and Confederate officers look on. Grant allowed Lee's men to retain their horses and rifles, as well as their dignity. After the signing, Grant responded to Lee's description of his tired and hungry army by providing rations for them.

★ ARMY OF THE POTOMAC

Many people in the Union initially felt the war would be as much entertainment as battle, over quickly and of little threat to northern troops. But the Battle of First Bull Run (Manassas) revealed a disorganized and ill-prepared Union force and a determined Confederate Army. Lincoln immediately called for the enlistment of five hundred thousand men for a three-year period. Volunteers from cities and farms throughout the North, most of whom had no experience fighting battles, crowded the training camps near Washington, DC. They would form the new Army of the Potomac.

The decisive first victory by the South at Bull Run made the North recognize that the war was real and that it must develop a much better fighting force. At the same time, it incorrectly led the South to assume that its troops were superior in battle.

Lincoln appointed a new commander, General George B. McClellan, who promised to transform the camps into organized, well-disciplined military bases; the troops into well-trained, prepared regiments; and the newly named Army of the Potomac into a force that could demonstrate superiority over the Confederates. McClellan successfully turned the civilian draftees into real soldiers and gained the unfailing admiration of the men he commanded.

During the course of war, fighting the enemy was not the only challenge faced by soldiers in the Army of the Potomac. The crowded, unsanitary conditions in the camps caused sickness and weakness among troops. Thousands died from typhoid fever, contracted from contaminated water. Thousands more caught malaria from mosquitoes that thronged men and animals. Lice and flea infestations were common. By 1862, virtually every man in the army—995 out of 1,000—suffered from dysentery. See *George Brinton McClellan*.

★ ATLANTA

The city of Atlanta, known for the iron arteries—railroads—that snaked their way throughout the South and connected the Confederacy, was a vital cog in the southern war machine. Without the rail links, the South would be paralyzed. The war could have ended much sooner if the Union armies had been able to cut off

Atlanta. In the end, when Sherman led the march to the sea that wiped out so much of the South, a primary mission for his men was to rip up rail, a task well orchestrated. They systematically went two by two with crowbars, prying up ties and pulling up track. They burned the ties and dumped the rail on top of the fire. When the rails were heated, the soldiers took the ends and twisted them into what became known as "Sherman's neckties." The sign of Union victory at the war's end was as much the collection of these iron neckties left throughout Georgia, as the gutted, empty buildings abandoned by fleeing civilians.

Atlanta, like so much of the South, was left in ruins. A key to the outcome of the war was halting rail shipments of food and supplies. Here the city and one of its major railroad facilities are shown totally destroyed.

★ BARTON, CLARA (1821–1912)

Clara Barton headed a major private relief effort to provide medicine and supplies to Union troops during the Civil War. The determined Barton, who owned her own school and was the first woman hired as a government employee in Washington, DC, was forty years old when the war began. Just two weeks later, she heard that several of her former students, now soldiers, had been injured by a pro-slavery mob. Seeing their condition and then watching the suffering when full-scale war began along Bull Run Creek near the city, she was convinced that something needed to be done to aid soldiers.

Before the U.S. Sanitary Commission was formed, Barton organized

LECTURE!

MISS CLARA BARTON,

OF WASHINGTON,

THE HEROINE OF ANDERSONVILLE,

The Soldier's Friend, who gave her time and fortune during the war to the Union cause, and who is now engaged in searching for the missing soldiers of the Union army, will address the people of

LAMBERTVILLE, in

HOLCOMBE HALL,

THIS EVENING,

APRIL 7TH, AT 7½ O'CLOCK.

SUBJECT:

SCENES ON THE BATTLE-FIELD.

ADMISSION,   25 CENTS.

warehouses to accept donations of supplies and personally directed a program to take wagonloads of goods directly to the battlefront and camps around Washington. She spent the entire Civil War collecting and distributing medical and other supplies. Known as the "angel of the battlefield," she always seemed to be wherever she was needed to remove bullets, bandage wounds, comfort soldiers, distribute supplies, or help however she could.

At the end of the war, Lincoln assigned Barton to lead the effort to search for missing soldiers. Later, in 1881, she founded the American Red Cross and devoted most of the remainder of her life to its growth and development as an international relief organization. See *U.S. Sanitary Commission*.

Clara Barton

★ BEAUREGARD, PIERRE GUSTAVE TOUTANT (1818–1893)

General P.G.T. Beauregard was one of many Civil War officers who had served in the Mexican War. When civil war appeared imminent, Beauregard resigned his commission in the U.S. Army to accept a similar position with the new Confederate Army, where one of his first tasks was to lead the bombardment of Fort Sumter, a federal

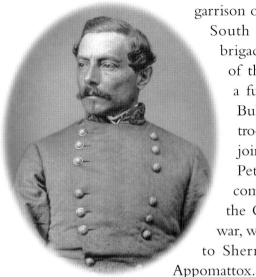

Pierre Gustave Toutant Beauregard

garrison on an island in the Charleston, South Carolina, harbor. He was a brigadier general at the beginning of the war but was promoted to a full general after the Battle of Bull Run. He was in charge of troops defending Charleston, then joined Lee in the defense of both Petersburg and Richmond. He commanded Confederate forces in the Carolinas until the end of the war, when he surrendered that army to Sherman after Lee's surrender at Appomattox.

★ BELLE ISLE PRISON

This Confederate prison in Richmond, Virginia, though less notorious than Andersonville Prison, was, like most Civil War prisons, overcrowded and terribly low on medical supplies and food. Belle Isle (and many other prisons) often fed prisoners as little as a spoonful of beans and a handful of corn a day. Water, when available, was full of bacteria. At the end of the war, nine out of every ten Union prisoners who left Belle Isle weighed less than one hundred pounds.

★ BLACK SOLDIERS

While white fears that black soldiers were inferior kept them out of battle for much of the war, black soldiers were increasingly important to the Union Army as the war progressed. They provided behind-the-lines support that allowed white soldiers to move to the front. After Lincoln's Emancipation Proclamation, the Union opened its ranks to blacks, who provided a vast supply of new recruits, something the South lacked. Finally, they were allowed to fight

under the command of white officers. "Nobody knows anything about these men who has not seen them in battle," wrote Thomas Wentworth Higginson about a group of South Carolina volunteers he led. The Massachusetts 54th, under the command of Robert Shaw, was perhaps the most famous black regiment because of its heroism at the Battle of Fort Wagner. But the 54th was just one of many black regiments throughout the latter days of the war whose bravery helped the North to victory.

★ BOOTH, JOHN WILKES (1838–1865)

A twenty-six-year-old actor and Confederate sympathizer, John Wilkes Booth entered President Lincoln's box at Ford's Theatre on April 14, 1865, and shot him at point-blank range. Booth, who was from a well-known family of actors, was a strong supporter of slavery and of the Confederacy, and he blamed President Lincoln for the South's problems. In March 1865, Booth came up with a plan to kidnap Lincoln and exchange him for Confederate pris-

Frederick Douglass wrote, "Why does the Government reject the Negro: Is he not a Man? Can he not wield a sword, fire a gun . . . ?" Here, two black Union soldiers are photographed "in action." But like white soldiers, they posed in simulated battle so photographers would not get a blurry image.

War Department, Washington. April 20, 1865.

$100,000 REWARD!
THE MURDERER

Of our late beloved President, ABRAHAM LINCOLN,

IS STILL AT LARGE.

$50,000 REWARD!

will be paid by this Department for his apprehension, in addition to any reward offered by Municipal Authorities or State Executives.

$25,000 REWARD!

will be paid for the apprehension of JOHN H. SURRATT, one of Booth's accomplices.

$25,000 REWARD!

will be paid for the apprehension of DANIEL C. HARROLD, another of Booth's accomplices.

LIBERAL REWARDS will be paid for any information that shall conduce to the arrest of either of the above-named criminals, or their accomplices.

All persons harboring or secreting the said persons, or either of them, or aiding or assisting their concealment or escape, will be treated as accomplices in the murder of the President and the attempted assassination of the Secretary of State, and shall be subject to trial before a Military Commission and the punishment of DEATH.

Let the stain of innocent blood be removed from the land by the arrest and punishment of the murderers.

All good citizens are exhorted to aid public justice on this occasion. Every man should consider his own conscience charged with this solemn duty, and rest neither night nor day until it be accomplished.

EDWIN M. STANTON, Secretary of War.

DESCRIPTIONS.—BOOTH is 5 feet 7 or 8 inches high, slender build, high forehead, black hair, black eyes, and wears a heavy black moustache. JOHN H. SURRATT is about 5 feet 9 inches. Hair rather thin and dark, eyes rather light, no beard. Would weigh 145 or 150 pounds. Complexion rather pale and clear, with color in his cheeks. Wore light clothes of fine quality. Shoulders square; cheek bones rather prominent; chin narrow; ears projecting at the top; forehead rather low and square, but broad. Parts his hair on the right side; neck rather long. His lips are firmly set. A slim man. DANIEL C. HARROLD is 22 years of age, 5 feet 6 or 7 inches high rather broad shouldered, otherwise light built; hair, dark, hair little (if any) moustache; dark eyes; weighs about 140 pounds.

GEO. F. NESBITT & CO., Printers and Stationers, cor. Pearl and Pine Streets, N. Y.

Booth was trapped and shot by a Union soldier shortly after this reward was offered.

oners. He put together a group of accomplices—Lewis Paine, George Atzerodt, David Herold, Samuel Arnold, Michael O'Laughlin, John Surratt, and Mary Surratt, who owned a boardinghouse in Washington where the conspirators often met. That plot failed because Lincoln changed his travel plans. Booth's friends said he felt his destiny was a place in history, and he hated "the tyrant."

After the surrender of the Confederacy, kidnapping the president would have been pointless, but Booth had no intention of giving up his plans; he changed his objective to murder. "Our country owed all our troubles to [Lincoln]," Booth wrote. "God . . . made me the instrument of his punishment." Booth heard that Lincoln would be at Ford's Theatre on April 14, to see a performance of *Our American Cousin*, and he plotted the murder for that night. He walked quietly into the president's private balcony box unnoticed, waited until loud laughter filled the theatre, and shot Lincoln once in the back of the head. Booth then jumped onto the stage, breaking his leg, but before anyone could follow he fled to a nearby alley and escaped on horseback. The country, at least the North, was incensed, and a massive manhunt followed. It was a week before Booth was trapped and shot in a nearby Virginia farmhouse.

After the shooting, Lincoln was carried to a boardinghouse across the street, where he died the next morning. Booth had directed Paine to kill Secretary of State William Seward, while Atzerodt was to shoot Vice President

Andrew Johnson. Only Booth succeeded, although Paine stabbed and seriously wounded Seward. Even Northern observers felt the conspirators had little chance of a fair trial. A quick verdict was handed down and four of the conspirators were hanged immediately.

★ BORDER STATES

The four "border" states between the Union and Confederate states were critical to the outcome of the Civil War. Maryland, Kentucky, Missouri, and Delaware permitted slavery, and many influential leaders in these four states wanted to join the South. But Lincoln at least wanted their neutrality if he could not have their support. He did all he could to ensure the border states did not secede. Maryland surrounded the city of Washington on three sides (Virginia bordered the capital on the other), and Kentucky was crucial for control of the Ohio River. Lincoln reportedly said that he *hoped* to have God on his side but *had to* have Kentucky. Abolitionists wanted slaves freed in these states, but Lincoln knew that freeing them would drive these states out of the Union. The Emancipation Proclamation was his answer. It freed no slaves in the North, where slavery did not exist; it freed the slaves in the South in areas of "rebellion," where Lincoln had no control; and it left the slaves alone in the border states, which then remained in the Union but continued their "neutral" stance.

★ BRADY, MATHEW (CA. 1823–1896)

The Civil War was the first war to be well documented by both reporters and photographers. Pictures of the battles and their aftermath—fields littered with thousands of corpses—explicitly showed what only paintings, drawings, and words had been available to describe before. The camera made the horrors of war—of the Civil War—painfully clear for everyone to see. Photographers set up studios and tents everywhere to take portraits of soldiers when they enlisted—or while they were traveling with the troops—so their families could have something to remember them by. When the war began, Mathew Brady was a well-known studio photographer in Washington, DC, and he quickly set out to photograph the Battle of Bull Run. He soon became the most famous of all Civil War photographers for both his battlefield images and studio portraits. Although many of his field photographs were actually taken by his assistants (he kept secret the fact that he was losing his sight), it was Brady's name that became synonymous with lasting images of the Civil War. In the North and to a lesser degree in the South, dozens of photographers worked throughout the war in both cities and tent studios. The images they created provide the earliest exhaustive photographic portrait of any war. The evolving art of photography had two major drawbacks, however: cumbersome equipment and long exposure time, which made actual battle photographs almost impossible. Photographers would often move corpses and pose scenes after the battle ended.

Photographers and sketch artists followed armies from battle to battle.

★ BRECKINRIDGE, JOHN C. (1821–1875)

A Confederate officer following a failed presidential campaign in 1860, John C. Breckinridge, of Kentucky, had previously served as vice president under President Buchanan. At that time, he was the youngest man ever to hold that office. He served as brigadier general in the Confederate Army, and from the summer of 1864 until the end of the war, he was the South's secretary of war. During the Battle of Atlanta, his own brother, Union officer W. C. Breckinridge, captured him. After the war he fled to Cuba, then to England, before returning to the United States in 1869. He practiced law in Kentucky until his death six years later.

★ BROWN, JOHN (1800–1859)

The fight over slavery was not a new one when the Civil War began. The debate had raged in Congress and in violent uprisings throughout the country for years. John Brown, a devout, fanatical abolitionist, was an unsuccessful businessman who had moved from state to state looking for work. At one time he operated a shelter for runaway slaves in Ohio. He also formed a society in New York that attempted to arm slaves to help them oppose the Fugitive Slave Law— a law that required government agents to help catch and return any black person known to be an escaped slave. Brown was in Kansas in 1856 when he heard that South Carolina Congressman Preston Brooks had savagely attacked abolitionist Senator Charles Sumner, beating him with a cane. Enraged, Brown organized a band of abolitionists intent on attacking pro-slavery Kansas residents; they succeeded in killing several people in a settlement along Pottawatomie Creek before U.S. troops stopped the violence.

Zealous in his abolitionist views, John Brown was so extreme he believed that his Harpers Ferry uprising would lead to an all-out slave revolt.

Three years later, still wanted for the Kansas murders, Brown led a poorly organized uprising at Harpers Ferry, Virginia, which he thought would be the beginning of a slave revolt. His plan was to capture the federal weapons supply house, and then wait for hundreds of slaves to break free from nearby plantations and join him in freeing southern slaves. No slaves rushed to join Brown's rebellion, and he was arrested and most of his men killed. Though Brown was tried and hanged for his crime, in some ways he succeeded: His death strengthened the abolitionist movement in the North. His actions also terrified many in the South, increasing their fears that slavery and the plantation way of life were under siege. A Richmond newspaper noted that "the Harpers Ferry invasion has advanced the cause of disunion more than any event that has happened since the formation of the government." See *Harpers Ferry, Virginia.*

★ BULL RUN, BATTLE OF (MANASSAS IN SOUTH)

Bull Run, a small Virginia creek near Washington, DC, was the site of one of the Civil War's earliest and bloodiest battles. Called "Manassas" by the South, after the rail junction where Confederate troops had assembled a few miles north of Bull Run, the battle took place on July 21, 1861. Hundreds of local residents, including society women dressed as if they were attending a garden party, came to watch from a nearby hill, convinced that the rebellion would be short-lived and end with an easy victory for the North. Few civilians could contemplate the vast horror that ultimately would result or the reality that 600,000 soldiers would die before the war's end. Many felt an urgency to see the battle at Bull Run, expecting that the war would begin and end right there. Instead, the South won a resounding victory, scattering the Union troops, who fled toward Washington ahead of the horrified spectators. A total of 1,025 men were killed and 2,550 wounded. The

Northerners gathered to picnic and watch the start and, they thought, the end of the little skirmish with the South. Troops and spectators ran in shock and disbelief. This was just the beginning of four years of the horrors of a war that Northerners simply assumed would be over in a matter of weeks.

Major Civil War Battles

MINNESOTA

WISCONSIN

MICHIGAN

IOWA

MAINE

VT

N.H.

NEW YORK

MASS

CONN R.I.

PENNSYLVANIA

GETTYSBURG
ANTIETAM
M.D.

N.J.

DEL.

Washington, D.C.

BULL RUN

FREDERICKSBURG
CHANCELLORSVILLE
WILDERNESS
SPOTSYLVANIA
COLD HARBOR
PETERSBURG

OHIO

ILLINOIS

INDIANA

WEST VIRGINIA

MISSOURI

KENTUCKY

VIRGINIA

Richmond

NORTH CAROLINA

TENNESSEE

FORT PILLOW

SHILOH

ARKANSAS

CORINTH

CHICKAMAUGA

SOUTH CAROLINA

Charleston FORT SUMTER

Atlanta

ALABAMA

GEORGIA

VICKSBURG

MISSISSIPPI

LOUISIANA
New Orleans

FLORIDA

©2001 Norman P. Bolotin/The History Bank

Bull Run, a small and overgrown river not far from Washington, DC, proved a terrible initiation for Civil War soldiers learning to fight the enemy as well as battling the terrain. Today, Bull Run looks much the same as it did then.

Confederates captured 1,200 Union soldiers. The romance of the war quickly disappeared, as did the idea that it would be over as quickly as it had started.

Second Bull Run was a far larger battle. Just a year after the first, the Union under General John Pope was soundly defeated, losing 16,000 men to Lee's 9,000.

★ BURNSIDE, AMBROSE EVERETT (1824–1881)

General Ambrose Burnside enjoyed great success, and suffered disheartening defeat, as a Union officer in the Civil War. Known as a brave but somewhat reckless leader, he was nicknamed "sideburns," to describe his interesting whiskers, which instead of forming a beard were thick at the sides, a bushy version of what are commonly called sideburns today. After Burnside led several successful battles, President Lincoln asked him to command the Army of the Potomac, a position he twice refused. Finally he relented, replacing George McClellan in November 1862. Just a month later, at Fredericksburg, Maryland, Burnside drove his troops straight into the heart of Lee's army and was soundly defeated. Burnside commanded 113,000 men, 35,000 more than he faced, but he suffered almost 13,000 casualties. He resigned from the command, but Lincoln reassigned him, and he later led troops in the battles of the Wilderness, Spotsylvania, and Petersburg.

★ CALHOUN, JOHN C. (1782–1850)

Though he died more than a decade before the Civil War began, John Calhoun has often been called the Father of Secession, even the Father of the Confederacy. Calhoun, a lawyer from South Carolina, was secretary of war under President Monroe and vice president for both John Quincy Adams and Andrew Jackson. While vice president, he sharply disagreed with Jackson and said that any state should be able to override a federal law if the new federal law changed a law that existed when the state was admitted to the Union. The issue was left in debate, and the country avoided what might have been a Civil War years earlier. Calhoun also served in the Senate, where he continued to battle for states' rights and was referred to as "The Napoleon of Slavery," endorsing slavery until his death in 1850.

John C. Calhoun

★ CARTE DE VISITE

Photography studios existed by the hundreds in small towns and large cities during the Civil War. The *carte de visite*—French for "visiting card"—was an inexpensive way for soldiers to send portraits home to family or friends, girlfriends or wives. A *carte de visite* looked much like a modern postcard, except it bore a photograph of the sender.

J. E. McCLEES,
ARTIST.
910 Chestnut Street,
PHILADELPHIA

CDVs are one of the most popular ways today to collect Civil War photos—much like collecting baseball cards. The "backmarks" indicate the photographer or studio and often its address.

CDVs were printed from glass negatives. For five dollars a soldier could have his picture taken and a dozen copies made. Most of the CDVs were made in studios (rather than by photographers in roving tents or wagons) equipped with elaborate backdrops to give the impression of battlefields, camps, ships, or boats. Photographers kept their own arsenal of weapons to embellish the pictures as well. Today, CDVs are one of the most widely collected forms of Civil War memorabilia.

⭐ CASUALTIES OF WAR

The casualties of the Civil War—those men killed, wounded, missing in action, or captured—were enormous as a percentage of the nation's population. Typically, in nineteenth-century warfare, the wounded far outnumbered the dead. Weapons were often inaccurate and unreliable, but they were also brutally effective in tearing apart whatever they did hit. Soft lead bullets could fill the air like swarms of deadly insects, ripping gruesome wounds wherever they struck. Battlefield amputations were the most common surgery, as the hospitals resembled slaughterhouses more than any kind of medical facility. Doctors, many with minimal training and no credentials, simply removed mangled limbs and tried to stop bleeding. Then the second war would begin—the battle to survive disease and infection. As an example, the Battle of Antietam resulted in 12,500 Union

Battlefield hospitals were often little more than amputation houses. Where nurses were available, battlefield survivors received care and attention, but the death rate from infection and lingering disease was high.

casualties. This included "only" 2,000 battlefield deaths, 9,500 wounded (countless of whom subsequently died or were permanently disabled), and 1,000 missing in action. Unfortunately, the intensity of Civil War battles, where as many as a quarter-million men engaged with one another within just a few square miles, resulted in hundreds or even thousands of men missing in action—unidentifiable from injuries, separated from their identification, or buried in hastily dug mass graves.

HOW DO YOU PICTURE 600,000 BATTLE DEAD?

Can you imagine just how many 600,000 people really are?

The Union and Confederate dead would fill 2,000 theaters, 13 major-league baseball stadiums, 10 typical pro football stadiums, six Super Bowl stadiums, or more than 1,000 elementary schools.

★ CHAMBERLAIN, JOSHUA LAWRENCE (1828–1914)

Commanding the 20th Maine Regiment at the Battle of Gettysburg was a thirty-three-year-old professor from Bowdoin College, Joshua Lawrence Chamberlain. His 386 men fought gallantly, defending a key hill called Little Round Top. They lost 130 men before eventually driving back a Confederate regiment twice their size, intent on taking the hill and then pushing through Union lines. Later,

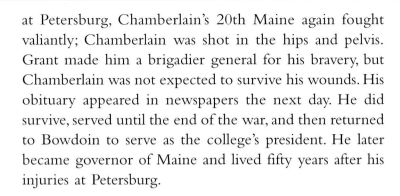

THE UNION ARMIES HAD AN ESTIMATED 2,500,000 TO 2,750,000 MEN IN UNIFORM DURING THE CIVIL WAR.

at Petersburg, Chamberlain's 20th Maine again fought valiantly; Chamberlain was shot in the hips and pelvis. Grant made him a brigadier general for his bravery, but Chamberlain was not expected to survive his wounds. His obituary appeared in newspapers the next day. He did survive, served until the end of the war, and then returned to Bowdoin to serve as the college's president. He later became governor of Maine and lived fifty years after his injuries at Petersburg.

CHAMBERSBURG, PENNSYLVANIA

The city of Chambersburg, Pennsylvania, was burned to the ground in July 1864 by Jubal Early and his men, in retaliation for similar actions by the Union Army moving through the South. Early demanded a half-million dollars in ransom to spare Chambersburg. When the citizens of the town refused to pay, he ordered the business district set on fire. Northerners feared that rampaging Confederate troops might conduct such raids even closer to Washington. After three years of fierce fighting between the North and South, and the critical defeat of the South in 1863 at Gettysburg, Pennsylvania, the raids had little military significance for the South, but they did inflict some losses and deepened the hatred between the two sides.

CHANCELLORSVILLE, BATTLE OF, VIRGINIA

The Battle of Chancellorsville, Virginia, was one of the bloodiest of the Civil War. General Joe Hooker led the Union forces, almost 134,000 strong, into battle in and around Chancellorsville. Lee had wintered there with an army of just 60,000, contemplating a campaign into Pennsylvania. Hooker was confident and pressed the attack on May 1, 1863, with heated battle continuing through May 4. Lee suffered 20 percent casualties—almost 13,000 of his men, but he defeated the vastly larger northern forces.

Hooker suffered more than 17,000 casualties. But the casualty that loomed the largest at Chancellorsville was one that ultimately contributed heavily to the South's defeat in the war. General Thomas "Stonewall" Jackson was mistaken for a Union rider and shot by Confederate troops. He died a week later. Lee considered Jackson his right hand, a hero to all the people of the South and a genius on the battlefield. Lee wrote about Jackson in his official record of the battle, "I desire to pay the tribute of my admiration to the matchless energy and skill that marked the last act of his life, forming, as it did, a worthy conclusion of that long series of splendid achievements which won him the lasting love and gratitude of his country." Lee said that the absence of Jackson two months later at Gettysburg could not be overstated. Chancellorsville and then Gettysburg demonstrated how much thinner the ranks of Lee's army were, and the fact that reinforcements were readily available for the North but not the South. The scarcity of experienced Confederate troops, from privates to experienced generals, only continued to grow as the war dragged on two more years.

Charleston was one of the major cities of the South where sentiment was strongly anti-North long before the war.

★ CHARLESTON, SOUTH CAROLINA

Fort Sumter, one of several forts defending Charleston harbor and the city of Charleston, was captured by the South in April 1861, marking the beginning of the Civil War. Throughout the war, the city of Charleston was considered the heart of the Confederacy. The Union Army and

MONTICELLO PUBLIC LIBRARY
512 E. LAKE AVE.
MONTICELLO, WI 53570

Charleston was bombarded constantly during the war, and by the time it was finally evacuated, most of the city was in ruins.

Navy bombarded it continuously in an attempt to capture it, but Charleston would not fall. The city was finally evacuated in February 1865 when William Tecumseh Sherman's army approached it during its march through South Carolina. Sherman's army destroyed almost everything in its path, but Charleston had already been devastated by years of continual shelling.

★ CHESNUT, MARY (1823–1886)

Many of the most vivid images of life during the Civil War came from the diaries and letters of soldiers and their families and friends back home. Mary Chesnut, who lived in the heart of the Confederacy, was one of the best-known diarists of the Civil War. Her wealthy, slave-holding father was a South Carolina congressman, senator, and governor. Her husband served as an aide to both General Beauregard and President Jefferson Davis, later becoming a general himself. Chesnut accompanied her husband to various battle sites, and the drawing room in her home often became a gathering place for the elite of the Confederacy. Her firsthand accounts chronicle how four years of death and destruction changed the South. She wrote of soldiers coming home with arms and legs and eyes missing; of friends hearing about the death of their husbands, fathers, and fiancés; of smallpox and scarlet fever ravaging her neighbors; of the fear of slaves rising up against their owners; and of the difficulty of surviving each day as it came, not knowing what new horrors Southerners would have to face. She portrayed a world where tea parties took place in palatial southern mansions while, only a carriage ride away, buildings were burning and people were dying. Chesnut wrote her diary in the hope that one day it would be used for historical purposes. She later edited her entries, and for well over one hundred years her diary has been everything she intended.

Mary Chesnut continued writing after the war, working on several novels that were never published. Then she went back to her diary to revise and expand it during the 1880s. She died in 1886, the diaries still unpublished. Finally, in 1905 a first edition was printed. Her posthumously reedited and published book is widely acknowledged as one of the best works written on the Confederacy.

★ CHICKAMAUGA, BATTLE OF

Fought September 19–20, 1863, near Chattanooga, Tennessee, the Battle of Chickamauga was the second-most costly battle of the Civil War in total casualties. More than 34,600 men—16,170 Union and 18,454 Confederate—were killed or wounded, many during fierce hand-to-hand combat. The Confederate troops under Braxton Bragg defeated Union troops led by William Rosecrans, but Bragg was either unwilling or unable to follow up his victory with a second assault. If not for a quick decision to withdraw by Union officer George Henry Thomas, the Union Army might have retreated to Chattanooga in even worse shape. Had Bragg made the decision to pursue the northern troops, the Confederates could have inflicted still more damage.

★ CIVIL WAR TOKENS

Because copper was needed to build ships and cannon for the war, the government ceased making most copper coins and merchants began coining their own replacement "pennies." They generally came in two types: "storecards," which advertised a business and were redeemable there as one cent; and "patriotics," which carried slogans supporting the war effort and sometimes had advertising on one side. Because of the shortage of pennies, both kinds of tokens were accepted as payment throughout the North, from business to business.

★ CLAY, HENRY (1777–1852)

Three times a loser in presidential elections, as a senator from Kentucky, Clay was a winner by all accounts in service to his country. He was known as the "Great Compromiser" after he orchestrated the Missouri Compromise (1820), which admitted Missouri as a slave state and admitted Maine as a free state, preserving the balance of power in Congress between the North and the South.

Clay's plan bought the country peace for more than twenty-five years, but war with Mexico threatened that domestic harmony. Arguments began over whether to allow slavery in the vast new territories won in the war. Clay, by then a very old man in declining health, returned with his skill as an orator to offer a new compromise on an old subject. He devised what came to be known as the Compromise of 1850 and was able to convince his northern and southern colleagues in the Senate once again to accept his ideas to avert political disaster or civil war. California was admitted as a free state,

Henry Clay

while the new states of Utah and New Mexico were given the authority to decide for themselves whether or not to permit slavery. Slave sales were outlawed in Washington, DC, and to appease the South, a tough Fugitive Slave Law was enacted. On the surface it may have seemed reasonable, until more violence erupted as slave hunters used the new law as authorization to beat, capture, or kill runaways, and even to claim any black person they "captured" was a runaway. See *States' Rights*.

CONFEDERATE RECORDS LACK DETAIL, BUT ESTIMATES OF TROOP STRENGTH RANGE FROM 750,000 TO 1,250,000.

 COLD HARBOR, BATTLE OF

Although the Battle of Cold Harbor (named for a nearby tavern that did not serve hot food) lasted three days, most of the fighting occurred in less than ten minutes. Robert E. Lee had entrenched his Confederate Army along the Chickahominy River near Richmond. Union Commander Ulysses Grant knew that a successful attack at Cold Harbor against Lee might mean victory—if he could drive Lee's army back and allow the Union troops to capture Richmond, the southern capital. Grant sent his men against Lee on June 3, 1864, but he had little optimism that they could defeat the Confederates: Lee's army had dug deep trenches for protection and built strong fortification lines to resist the onrushing Union soldiers.

Lee's men fired hundreds of thousands of rounds into the Union troops as they rushed the stronghold, resulting in the bloodiest minutes of the Civil War. Grant's troops not only failed to overrun the trenches, but suffered seven thousand casualties—dead and wounded—in that horrific eight-minute attack. Confederate losses were fifteen hundred.

One Confederate survivor described the scene right after the battle: "The dead covered more than five acres of ground about as thickly as they could be laid." For two days after the failed attack, both sides sat and waited, refusing to ask for a truce to recover bodies or tend to the wounded. On the third day, each side relented and began moving forward to look for survivors and to bury their dead. The attack at Cold Harbor was the single mistake Grant admitted to making during his time as a Union general.

As horrific as the battle was, generals in both armies were painfully accustomed to such carnage. In sending their daily reports to their respective War Departments, Lee and Grant had little to say at the time. Grant and Meade cited losses that were "severe," while Lee said, "our loss today has been small, and our success . . . all that we could expect."

★ COMPROMISE OF 1850

Senator Henry Clay of Kentucky did not want to see the conflict over slavery break up the Union. Clay was known as a superior orator, clever politician, and talented actor on his stage, the speaker's podium in the Senate. He came up with a compromise to try to satisfy both the North and the South and prevent war. Clay's Compromise of 1850 allowed California to enter the United States as a free state, but in exchange let the new states of Utah and New Mexico decide for themselves whether or not to allow slavery. The Compromise also abolished the sale of slaves in Washington, DC, but offered Southerners something in exchange—a strong Fugitive Slave Law. Federal agents anywhere were now required to help capture runaway slaves, and it became a criminal offense for ordinary citizens to aid runaways.

Clay was not able to avert war, only to postpone it for the next decade. Though he was in his seventies and in poor health, for three hours his passion mesmerized the Senate as he appealed to his colleagues to behave rationally to save the Union. See *Henry Clay*.

A very early photo of Confederate troops in Charleston. The flag has just seven stars representing the first seven states to secede. Also, the Confederate troops are in full and new uniforms, something rarely seen later in the war as the Confederate government struggled to provide adequate food, ammunition, and supplies.

★ CONFEDERATE STATES OF AMERICA

The eleven states that withdrew, or seceded, from the Union between December 20, 1860, and early 1861, formed the Confederate States of America. Their plan was to establish a completely separate nation. These states believed in strong states' rights, including their right to allow slavery, issues which had been hotly contested in the U.S. Congress and the Senate for decades. South Carolina was the first to secede, and by April 12, 1861, when Fort Sumter was fired on, six other states—Alabama, Florida, Georgia, Louisiana, Mississippi, and Texas—had also seceded. Within a month they were joined by Arkansas, North Carolina, Tennessee, and Virginia.

The federal government looked upon these states as "rebels" that were still governed by the laws of the United States, but the Confederate government made it clear they considered themselves a separate country. The new Confederacy wasted no time in establishing its own government, electing Jefferson Davis as its president, creating a war department, forming a treasury, seeking recognition from foreign countries, and more. It printed its own money and drafted its own constitution. Jefferson Davis was inaugurated president of the Confederate States of America on February 18, 1861.

★ CONTRABAND

Runaway slaves seeking refuge at Union camps became known as "contrabands," or, as General Benjamin Butler first noted for the North, "contrabands of war"—captured enemy property, and therefore not to be returned to their southern owners. Contraband camps became common near Union troops in Confederate territory. Contrabands were given menial or even hard labor tasks to support the army. More than a half-million former slaves became contrabands, some toiling years for no wages, others feeling they had reached a promised land, and still others bitter over the harsh treatment they found at the hands of Northerners. "On every face there was a look of serenity," observed black teacher Charlotte Forten, commenting on escaping slaves she had helped, but for former slave Elizabeth Keckly, commenting on the plight of both

Contrabands were often put to work by Union officers, doing washing, cooking, and even hard labor. Here, a group of contrabands washes clothing for the troops.

contrabands and former southern slaves living as free men and women in the North, it was just the opposite. "The North is not warm and impulsive," she said. "For one kind word spoken, two harsh ones were uttered."

★ COPPERHEADS

Copperheads were a northern faction of the Democratic party that did not support the Civil War. Their opponents, who believed it was necessary to fight for the Union and against slavery, named them after the venomous snake to emphasize how "poisonous" to the Union cause the Copperheads' beliefs were. Many Copperheads took the nickname as a compliment, however, campaigning against a war they claimed killed thousands of people yet did nothing to free slaves. Southerners did all they could to support the Copperheads, who wanted the

North to end the war unilaterally. Lincoln was unwavering in his opinion of the Copperheads. He felt they undermined Union efforts by encouraging soldiers to desert "in the name of peace."

★ CUSTER, GEORGE ARMSTRONG (1839–1876)

While best remembered for his Indian-fighting exploits in the post-Civil War westward expansion, George Armstrong Custer distinguished himself as a cavalry leader during the war. When the war began, Custer was in his fourth year at West Point, where, despite his obvious intelligence, he graduated last in his class. In the early days

Union officers share a peaceful moment and a pipe of tobacco in the field. The young lieutenant in the foreground, with the dog, is George Armstrong Custer, looking unusually nonflamboyant.

"I HAVE SLEPT IN CORN CRIBS, HENHOUSES, WAGON HOUSES . . . AND ONE HOG PEN."

"Well, my dear fellow, the whole thing has gone up! No more camp for us, no more separations. Four years ago Fort Sumter was besieged by a set of traitorous villains who if they could see the consequences of what was to follow, would have sunk into the sandbars of South Carolina without even a pebble to mark their ignominious resting place. With the exception of two days, my health has been of the first order ever since leaving the far off "Vale of the Shenandoah." Just seven months and one day from the time that I was mustered into the US service, I witnessed the surrender of General Lee. I was a lucky fellow to be there to see it. I shall try to visit Richmond and Petersburg soon. I was walking very leisurely on my horse through Dinwiddie County about four o'clock in the PM one fine day when a courier came rushing up and said, "Richmond is ours!" I shall always remember the exact spot where I heard this news. Just 800 miles I have booked since Winchester, and you would hardly know your pale-faced cousin in the brown, full face of I. Yet I carry the same eyes and same color hair and brows, but how changed for I look like a veteran of the "Gold Diggers." But, Thomas, the same heart beats within me, and it beats warmly for friends and family. I can remember a few things that might amuse you. I have slept in corn cribs, henhouses, wagon houses, sheds, granary houses, and one hog pen. I have laid
among pine, cedar, and oak woods some of the time dry, and some of the time with clothes and blankets wringing wet. I had a shell burst close to me a few days ago, and a piece came too close to my head for safe feelings. I have had bullets fly all about me thickly. One came close to my upper lip (probably wanted my mustache!); another came close to my left hand but I heeded them not. Why should I, they were not meant for me. I could not stay back for how could I see anything by hiding, and my Yankee curiosity sent me ahead invariably. The heavy fighting of the 6th inst. I witnessed the whole of at Saylor's Creek. Our Division captured 32 rebel flags. Also the Battle of Five Forks was a hard one as was the Battle at Dinwiddie Court House where I was up where the lead came uncomfortably close. The next day we captured about 6000 prisoners. I have a very pretty sword and belt which doesn't belong to the US government and which I mean to take home. It is rapidly growing dark. With promises to write again, I will close by professing that I am Very truly yours, N. Albert Sherman. Direct to N. Albert Sherman, Hd Qtrs. Cav M.M.D. Washington, D.C. Gen'l Custer is in command of the Cav. Corps."*

Sherman, a young man during the war, lived another fifty-five years after he wrote the description of the war's end, passing away in 1920 in Nebraska.

of the fighting, Custer served on the staffs of Generals McClellan and Pleasonton, and then rose to a more powerful position when George Meade became the new head of the Army of the Potomac. Meade appointed Custer one of three new captains. Leading the Michigan Brigade, Custer distinguished himself with a victory over Jeb Stuart's much larger force at Gettysburg. A flamboyant, self-confident figure, Custer was always at the front of his troops—as much for excitement and attention as anything else. To ensure that reporters would not miss him, he wore a gold-trimmed "uniform" he had specially tailored, which made him look more like a seventeenth-century European count than a nineteenth-century Union soldier. His exploits and victories continued through the war, and in the decade following the war, his reputation brought him continued notoriety and controversy during what was known as the Indian Wars. He died with the same flamboyance as he exhibited in the Civil War and the years fighting Indians in the West. At Little Big Horn, his poor tactics and arrogance led to the annihilation of every one of his two hundred men as well as himself. For many years referred to as a hero, Custer later came to epitomize the ultimate example of brutal and misguided treatment of Native Americans.

D

The man who became president of the Confederate States of America did not seek that position. He was selected by the new Congress of the Confederacy. During the 1850s, Jefferson Davis had served as a U.S. senator from Mississippi and also as the U.S. secretary of war under President Franklin Pierce. Like Lincoln, Davis was born in a Kentucky log cabin, but his family soon moved to cotton country in Mississippi. Two hallmarks of his career were his belief not only in the continuation, but the expansion, of slavery, and his belief that compromise should seldom, if ever, be a first course of action. Davis was very confident, and he was closely involved in the direction of the Confederate Army throughout the war but as the war dragged on, the strain showed in the lines and exhaustion on his face. Viewed by southern leaders as fair and sensitive, Davis had a reputation as a moderate slaveowner. On his own plantation, he seldom was involved in direct management of slaves, but that was not

Jefferson Davis

left to white overseers. Rather a special court of fellow slaves determined appropriate punishment. After the war, Davis was arrested by the federal government and imprisoned for treason. Horace Greeley and others posted a one-hundred-thousand-dollar bond for Davis's release, much to the displeasure of many Northerners.

★ DIX, DOROTHEA (1802–1887)

Dorothea Dix

Dorothea Dix, known as "Dragon Dix" for her stern demeanor, was vitally important to the survival of tens of thousands of Union soldiers. Before the war, Dix worked for several decades to improve conditions for patients in mental hospitals. When war broke out, Dix, at age fifty-nine, volunteered for the Union cause and was put in charge of recruiting women to serve as nurses in the Army Medical Bureau, where a corps of three thousand women endured the same terrible conditions as soldiers in order to provide much-needed medical care. Responsible for improving the quality of wartime health care, this "Superintendent of Female Nurses" was strict in all aspects of her work, announcing that no women who were attractive, under thirty, or looking for romance need apply. She wanted them "plain-looking" and middle-aged. Perseverance and hard work alone mattered. After the war, Dix returned to the reform work she had pioneered—improving the treatment of mentally ill. She considered her service for the army a minor episode in her life, "not the work I would have me judged by."

★ DOUBLEDAY, ABNER (1819–1893)

Captain Abner Doubleday was in charge of the artillery at Fort Sumter when the war began, and it was he whose men fired the first shots in defense of the fort when it was

attacked by the South. Promoted to general, Doubleday fought at Fredericksburg, Chancellorsville, Second Bull Run, and Antietam, and briefly held a command position at Gettysburg. He was nicknamed "Old Forty-eight Hours" because he was said to act as if he had that many hours in a day to make decisions. He was removed from command after Gettysburg.

Many historians credit Doubleday with inventing the game of baseball in his hometown of Cooperstown, New York. Other historians, including many baseball experts, disagree. He is known to have played the game both before and during the war, and today Cooperstown is home to Doubleday Field and the Baseball Hall of Fame.

Abner Doubleday

The 48th New York Infantry (in the background) play a game of baseball during the Civil War. Baseball was played often during the war, yet photos of it are quite rare.

★ DOUGLAS, STEPHEN (1813–1861)

A lawyer and statesman, Stephen Douglas (nicknamed "the Little Giant" for his small stature and great oratorical ability) reopened the issue of slavery in 1854 with his Kansas–Nebraska bill, which included a provision allowing these two territories to vote whether or not slavery should be permitted within their borders. Perhaps he is best known for his debates with Abraham Lincoln during their cam-

Stephen Douglas

paigns in Illinois in 1858 for U.S. Senate. Douglas won that election, but Lincoln gained notoriety from the "Great Debates," which led directly to his Republican nomination in 1860. Douglas's Freeport Doctrine was named for the site of the Lincoln-Douglas debate in which Douglas vehemently supported the rights of territories to determine if slavery would be allowed. The issue ultimately caused a split in the Democratic party. Pro-slavery Southerners supported a third candidate, John Breckinridge, in 1860 cutting into Douglas's votes. The result was a Republican victory for Abraham Lincoln. Douglas was disheartened by his failure in the presidential election but supported Lincoln as the war began. Not yet fifty, he died in 1861 of typhoid fever. See *Lincoln-Douglas Debates*.

> "CAN THE PEOPLE OF A TERRITORY IN ANY LAWFUL WAY, AGAINST THE WISHES OF ANY CITIZEN OF THE UNITED STATES, EXCLUDE SLAVERY FROM THEIR LIMITS PRIOR TO THE FORMATION OF A STATE CONSTITUTION? MR. LINCOLN HAS HEARD ME ANSWER A HUNDRED TIMES . . . THE PEOPLE . . . CAN."
>
> —*Stephen Douglas, Freeport Doctrine, 1858*

★ DOUGLASS, FREDERICK (1818–1895)

One of the most articulate and respected black men of the Civil War era was writer, abolitionist, and publisher Frederick Douglass, a former slave. Douglass had been a relatively fortunate slave in that he was taught to read and write by Sophia Auld, the wife of Hugh Auld, whom Douglass had been sent to serve in Baltimore. After escaping from slavery in 1838, he met William Lloyd Garrison and began speaking for the Massachusetts Anti-Slavery Society. To defend himself against accusations that such an eloquent man could not have recently escaped from slavery, Douglass wrote his autobiography, now a classic of American literature. He also published passionate articles against slavery in his newspaper, *North*

Frederick Douglass

Charles R. (left) and Lewis H. Douglass, Frederick's sons, fought with the 54th Massachusetts.

"DOUGLASS . . . ONLY NINE YEARS OUT OF BONDAGE, AND NOW WE FIND HIM ISSUING ONE OF THE ABLEST PAPERS IN THE UNION. WHO SAYS THE COLORED RACE IS INFERIOR IN INTELLECT?"

—*Hampshire Herald*

Star. Douglass continually reminded those to whom he spoke that it was useless to fight against slaveholders without also fighting against slavery itself. The only victory for the North would come with a victory for all men.

Douglass believed that blacks should have the right to fight in the Civil War. "Why does the Government reject the Negro: Is he not a man?" Douglass asked. "Can he not wield a sword, fire a gun, march and countermarch, and obey orders like any other . . . ?" Douglass told blacks that although they might have escaped slavery and found a life for themselves in the North, they were still treated like second-class citizens. Serving in the military would offer them a chance to both fight against slavery and to prove their equality with white Americans. After the Emancipation Proclamation took effect on January 1, 1863, Douglass was instrumental in helping recruit black soldiers.

★ EARLY, JUBAL ANDERSON (1816–1894)

Called "Old Jube" by his men even though he was not yet fifty years old during the war, Early was considered by Robert E. Lee one of his most competent generals. He was both modest in victory and undeterred by defeat. In July 1864, Early's troops reached the outskirts of Washington before being driven back. He marched into Pennsylvania and demanded a half-million-dollar ransom from the town of Chambersburg on July 30, 1864; when he didn't receive it, his troops took supplies and burned much of the town to the ground. Accused of savagery, he pointed out to the people of Chambersburg that while it was indeed unfortunate that war caused such things, what he had done was not very different from what the Union Army had been doing in the South for months. When Union troops destroyed the Virginia Military Institute, Early retaliated by burning Union Postmaster General Montgomery Blair's house in Maryland. Though Early often fought in situations where his troops were severely outnumbered, Ulysses Grant still considered him a serious enough threat to the Union to want him stopped. Early finally suffered serious defeats by Sheridan and then by Custer as the war neared an end. After the war, refusing to take an oath of allegiance to the United States, he fled to Mexico. He later returned and spent nearly thirty years as an attorney in the South.

★ EMANCIPATION PROCLAMATION

Abraham Lincoln issued the Emancipation Proclamation, freeing all slaves in the areas "in rebellion against the United States," on September 22, 1862. It became law January 1, 1863. It did nothing in the North, where slavery was already illegal. It also did nothing in the controversial four border states between the North and South, since they were not "in rebellion." But it did free the slaves in the Confederate states, where, from the South's point of view, Lincoln had no authority because of secession. Thus some historians argued that it was a hollow proclamation, yet it did result in tens of thousands of slaves fleeing to freedom, many of whom joined the Union Army. Lincoln felt that the permanent end of slavery could only be accomplished with a constitutional amendment. He fought hard to push the Thirteenth Amendment through Congress and is widely credited with the perseverence and political savvy that resulted in the victory.

From the Emancipation Proclamation

"On the first day of January, in the year of our Lord one thousand eight hundred and sixty three, all persons held as slaves within any State, or designated part of a State, the people whereof shall then be in rebellion against the United States, shall be then, thenceforth, and forever free."

★ ERICSSON, JOHN (1803–1889)

John Ericsson was a Swedish-born inventor who is best known for designing the *Monitor,* a Union ironclad gunboat. In 1861, rumors reached the Union Navy that the Confederates were beginning work on converting the *Merrimack,* a former frigate, to an ironclad warship. Gideon Welles, Lincoln's secretary of the navy, enlisted Ericsson to build an ironclad gunboat for the Union Navy. Ericsson had first devised his plan for a partially submerged ironclad ship decades earlier, but both the English and the French had rejected his plans. After Welles's invitation, Ericsson took his vessel design from the drawing board to an ocean test in just three and a half months. The *Monitor* met the *Merrimack* in battle on March 9, 1862, and neither was able to defeat the other. Navies around the world realized that the ironclad design was an engineering revolution that would render their fleets of wooden vessels obsolete.

Ericsson will always be recognized for his ironclad design, but he was also a brilliant engineer who developed the more intricate workings of the ship. Although iron-

Perhaps the most famous of the Confederate ships was the **Virginia,** *the former U.S. frigate* **Merrimack,** *which was converted into an armored gunboat, known as an "ironclad." The* **Virginia** *(shown here attacking a Union supply vessel) posed a significant threat to northern ships, but the Union soon built its own ironclad—the* **Monitor**—*and the two vessels faced each other in the world's first modern sea battle. While both sides claimed victory, the* **Virginia** *was permanently disabled; it never again attacked Union ships.*

clad vessels had been built before, the *Monitor* was unique in many respects. Most of the boat rode completely underwater, with the flat deck floating only slightly more than a foot above the surface. It was propelled by one of Ericsson's inventions—the screw propeller—which was located below the waterline, thus safely protected from enemy fire. In fact, Ericsson's design of the *Monitor* included more than forty patentable inventions. See *Monitor and Merrimack.*

★ EVERETT, EDWARD (1794–1865)

Edward Everett was a famous orator and the former governor of Massachusetts when he was invited to be the keynote speaker at the dedication of the new national cemetery at Gettysburg on November 19, 1863.

Everett, seventy years old at the time, gave a nearly two-hour speech that day and was followed at the podium by President Lincoln, who rose to give "a few appropriate remarks," a speech now known as the Gettysburg Address. Some of the press reported the president's remarks as "dull and commonplace" compared with Everett's speech, but Everett noted the simple, touching brilliance of Lincoln's words, saying he wished he could have come "as near the central idea of the occasion" in two hours as Lincoln did in two minutes.

Everett had been a vice-presidential candidate in 1860, running with wealthy slaveowner John Bell against Lincoln. Bell and Everett were part of the "Constitutional Union" party, one that refused to take sides between the North and South, but instead recognized only the principles of the Constitution as its political platform. But their ticket, winning less than 3 percent of the northern vote, did not prove a serious threat to Lincoln. See *Gettysburg Address.*

Edward Everett

★ FARRAGUT, DAVID GLASGOW (1801—1870)

Some men in the Civil War became famous for bravery in battle or survival in conditions of extraordinary hardship. David Farragut earned his fame and place in naval history for his words rather than his actions. "Damn the torpedoes. Full speed ahead!" he shouted, leading his naval force against the Confederates at Mobile Bay, Alabama. The torpedoes to which he referred were what today are called "mines," devices in the water that explode on contact. A Union ship had been sunk and Farragut took his ship through a minefield to engage the enemy. After the war, Farragut gained more notoriety as the U.S. Navy's first admiral.

★ FORD'S THEATRE

Forever a part of American history, Ford's Theatre, located in the center of Washington, DC, was the site of President Lincoln's assassination on April 14, 1865. Lincoln, his wife, and two guests were watching a performance of the play *Our American Cousin* when John Wilkes Booth, an actor and Confederate supporter, entered their private box and shot the president in the back of the head.

After Lincoln's assassination, the Ford's Theatre building was used at various times as an office building, mu-

THE NORTH SUFFERED MORE THAN 110,000 BATTLE DEATHS, BUT MORE THAN 250,000 DEATHS FROM DISEASE AND OTHER CAUSES. THE SOUTH, BASED ON INCOMPLETE RECORDS, SUFFERED AN ESTIMATED 94,000 BATTLE DEATHS AND 164,000 NONBATTLE DEATHS.

seum, library, and warehouse. Today a popular tourist attraction, Ford's Theatre is a National Historic Site, offering dramatizations and information about its place in American history. See *John Wilkes Booth*.

FORREST, NATHAN BEDFORD (1821–1877)

One of the most surprising military stories of the war was that of Nathan Bedford Forrest, who enlisted as a private in the Confederate Army at the start of the war and rose to general by the end of the war. William Tecumseh Sherman called him "the most remarkable man" produced on either side. Before the war, Bedford was a wealthy slave trader in Tennessee. When war broke out, he used his own money to form a military unit. It was not unusual for a wealthy man to pay enlistees a bonus, pay for their uniforms, and then deliver them to the army as an entire fighting unit.

Known for his fiery temper and daring maneuvers, Forrest had a reputation throughout the North as one of the most dangerous cavalry raiders, attacking Union posts and fleeing before he could be captured. In one of the ugliest incidents of the war, the defeat of the Union garrison at Fort Pillow, his troops massacred hundreds of surrendering black troops, along with a smaller number of white soldiers. Forrest survived war injuries and an attack by one of his own men, as well as having several horses shot out from under him in battle. When the war was over, he contemplated taking his entire unit and fleeing to Mexico rather than surrendering. In the end, however, he ordered them to return to the reunited Union, "obey the laws," and rebuild the South. Forrest became a railroad executive and a plantation owner and died at fifty-six years of age in 1877.

FORT MOULTRIE

If not for one officer's hasty decision, Fort Moultrie might have been the fort attacked by the South that started the

The U.S. detachment at Fort Moultrie slipped away in the night, fearing an attack from organizing Southerners. But the detachment occupying nearby Fort Sumter only enraged southern leaders. Civil War was imminent.

Civil War. One of three outdated and undermanned forts in the harbor of Charleston, South Carolina, Moultrie was guarded by only a small group of Union soldiers who feared the worst: an attack by the rebel soldiers of South Carolina. Major Robert Anderson, in command of the fort, requested—indeed begged—for support from Washington but was ignored. So he decided he had no choice but to abandon Fort Moultrie without orders from his commanders. During the night, he secretly moved his men by rowboat to the better-protected Fort Sumter, in the middle of the harbor. It was at Fort Sumter that Anderson's garrison, still without provisions or reinforcements from Washington, was fired upon in what proved to be the start of the Civil War.

★ FORT PILLOW, TENNESSEE

On April 12, 1864, General Nathan Bedford Forrest's Confederate cavalry overran Fort Pillow on the Mississippi River, fifty miles upriver from Memphis. The Union soldiers, most of whom were black, were forced to surrender. Forrest's men, outraged at seeing that they were fighting black men, murdered many of the prisoners, both black and white. Southern sentiment ran high against

Jefferson Davis ignored the accepted rules of war and of human decency when it came to black Union soldiers—kill them or reenslave them. Fort Pillow further enraged Northerners as newspapers shouted the news: "The Massacre at Fort Pillow," "Three Hundred Black Soldiers Murdered After Surrender," and "Retaliation to Be Made."

former slaves, or any black men for that matter, taking up arms against the South. The Confederacy made it clear that any captured black soldier was considered under sentence of death.

★ FORT SUMTER

On April 12, 1861, the Civil War began with a Confederate attack on Fort Sumter in the Charleston, South Carolina, harbor. Fort Sumter was built on a man-made island of stone blocks in the center of the entrance to the harbor, an important position for control of the area. Months earlier, South Carolina, along with several other states, had voted to secede from the United States and create an independent nation. The leaders of South Carolina saw the U.S. Army's presence at Fort Sumter as a challenge to the independence of their new nation. Thus possession of Fort Sumter intensified the political tension between the United States and the emerging Confederate states. When the U.S. soldiers manning Fort Sumter began to run out of food in early April 1861, President Lincoln was faced with a crisis. Should he withdraw the men from the fort as a conciliatory gesture? Should he resupply and reinforce the fort at all costs? Finally, Lincoln decided to send provisions only. In an attempt to avoid war, he notified the governor of South Carolina that no soldiers or weapons would be on the relief ship. However, the newly formed Confederate government refused to allow any ships near Fort Sumter. Instead, they demanded immediate surrender of the fort and evacuation of all U.S. military forces from the area.

When Robert Anderson, commander of the small garrison of sixty-eight men defending the fort, refused to surrender, the Confederate commander General P.G.T. Beauregard ordered an attack. Several thousand troops bombarded Fort Sumter with heavy cannon. The battle lasted only two days, leaving the severely damaged fort in flames before Anderson surrendered to Beauregard. Thou-

April 12, 1861, the shelling of Fort Sumter started . . . and with it the Civil War.

sands of southern civilians witnessed this first battle of the war, in which not one casualty was suffered on either side. Neither South Carolina citizens nor the Union and Confederate soldiers had even a hint of the terrible devastation and death that was to follow in the next four years.

★ FREDERICKSBURG, BATTLE OF

The Battle of Fredericksburg, Virginia, December 11–15, 1862, took place three months after the Union victory at Antietam. Lincoln hoped to see his troops take the advantage in the war, which had already lasted much longer than most Northerners had expected. Lincoln placed Ambrose Burnside in command of the Army of the Potomac, replacing General George McClellan, whom Lincoln felt had not been aggressive enough in pursuing Lee's army after Antietam. Lincoln believed McClellan's hesitation had cost the Union forces the advantage they had earned at Antietam.

But at Fredericksburg, Burnside's 113,000 men could not defeat Lee's 75,000 troops. Lee had positioned his army on the hills overlooking Fredericksburg. The Union Army crossed the Rappahannock River, ransacked the town, and then moved forward to attack the southern defensive lines. They tried repeatedly to break through the southern strongholds, and each time they failed, cut down by the hundreds by the well-positioned Confederate troops. One in nine men under Burnside's command was dead or wounded before the general finally decided it was hopeless, and retreated. The Confederate casualties at Fredericksburg were high (5,000), but two and a half times higher (13,000) for the badly beaten Union forces.

★ FREEDMEN'S BUREAU

In March 1865, the federal government established the Bureau of Refugees, Freedmen and Abandoned Lands. The Bureau's offices throughout the South provided both blacks and whites with food, clothing, and fuel to survive the post-war economic devastation and helped former slaves with the transition to freedom. It was staffed primarily by soldiers, who had the difficult task of keeping peace when they often were helping both former masters and their slaves. Printed flyers or "broadsides" were posted and handed out to former slaves and slaveowners to inform them of their new rights and responsibilities, though few of those for whom they were intended could read. "The Negro has become free," one poster announced. "He is human, and is entitled to all the rights of a man." The period of rebuilding the country, its cities, and its societies was known as Reconstruction, and it was a terrible struggle for many years.

The Bureau of Refugees, Freedmen and Abandoned Lands also served as mediator when a disagreement arose between employers and employees (former slaves).

★ FRÉMONT, JOHN CHARLES (1813–1890)

Before the Civil War, John C. Frémont taught mathematics aboard navy ships and led several expeditions with army engineers to explore and map western regions of North America. After the Mexican War, he was appointed governor of California, later served as a senator from the state, and unsuccessfully ran for president of the United States in 1856. When the Civil War began, Lincoln appointed Frémont to the highest rank in the army, major general. Frémont took it upon himself to declare martial law in Missouri and issue his own "emancipation proclamation" for the state, freeing all slaves owned by southern sympa-

NEGRO UNION TROOPS SUFFERED 20 PERCENT CASUALTIES DURING THE WAR—36,000 OF ALMOST 179,000.

thizers. This infuriated Lincoln not only because the general did not have the authority to free slaves but because he feared it would anger the border states. Frémont was relieved of his duty and reassigned to track Stonewall Jackson's army in the Shenandoah Valley, but he was unsuccessful in locating it. After the war, he served as governor of Arizona from 1878 to 1882 and was reappointed major general of the army in 1890 when he was seventy-seven years old.

FUGITIVE SLAVE LAW

Henry Clay included a strengthened Fugitive Slave Law in his Compromise of 1850 in an attempt to appease southern slaveholders. It required any government agent to return a slave known to be a fugitive, and it fined any citizen one thousand dollars plus six months in jail for helping a fugitive slave. Southern slave hunters indiscriminately captured any black men or women they could, free or slave, in the North or South, then took them to the South for a reward. In response to the violence and lawlessness of the slave hunters, the northern abolitionist movement gained support and strength. Theodore Parker, an abolitionist leader who abhorred violence, wrote a letter to then President Millard Fillmore that summed up the situation throughout the country. "I will do all in my power to rescue any fugitive slave," he said. "What is a fine of a thousand dollars, and jailing for six months, to the liberty of a man?" Ironically, South Carolina cited the failure of fugitive slave laws in the North as one reason for secession. See *Henry Clay*.

★ GARRISON, WILLIAM LLOYD (1805–1879)

One of the most influential antislavery voices in the North was William Lloyd Garrison's. In 1831, the year that slave Nat Turner led a bloody revolt, Garrison, age twenty-five, began publishing an abolitionist newspaper, *The Liberator,* in Boston. A pacifist, Garrison wrote that abolishing slavery was even more important than winning the Civil War and that it was better to let the slaveholding states secede. While Garrison's ideas were considered extreme by many, his newspaper was widely read among abolitionists, and his stories were printed by other newspapers in the North and South. At one point, free black men were forbidden to accept delivery of *The Liberator* at the post office. Because the government said that the U.S. Constitution protected slavery where it already existed, Garrison burned a copy of the document in public, calling it "an agreement with hell."

William Lloyd Garrison

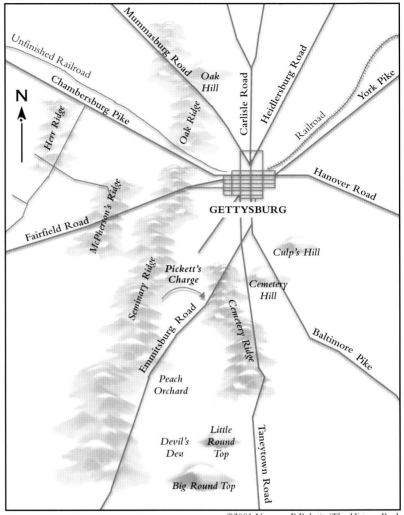

©2001 Norman P. Bolotin/The History Bank

★ GETTYSBURG, BATTLE OF

The most famous battle of the Civil War was fought in Gettysburg, a small town in Pennsylvania. It began over shoes and ended as the Civil War's bloodiest encounter and a critical turning point in the war.

Southern troops had been pushing northward in the summer of 1863 and for the first time were moving toward the heart of the Union. If the troops could march to western Pennsylvania, then turn back to the east, they would be in a perfect position to attack Philadelphia and New York, as well as threatening Washington, all from within the Union.

Rumors that there was a supply of shoes in Gettysburg, which was a main rail line, brought southern scouts into the city. Union leaders did not know where General Robert E. Lee and his army were located but suspected they were heading north and were somewhere in Pennsylvania. And Lee did not know where the Union's major stronghold of troops was, either, as he moved toward Gettysburg. When Lee and his sixty-five thousand men began fanning out through the fields near Gettysburg and into the town, there was only minimal gunfire from a small number of Union troops nearby. Neither side had any indication of what was to follow. Union troops were much closer and in dramatically larger numbers than Lee had expected. Unknown to both sides, a total of 150,000 men—northern and southern troops—were within marching distance of Gettysburg, and the two sides were moving closer to each other.

On July 1, 1863, the first major battle began just south of Gettysburg. The Union had vastly superior artillery all along what would become defensive positions against the attacks of massing Confederate troops to the south. The conflict was like a massive chess game, with northern artillery positions fortifying strongholds and the South moving along the flanks (side to side rather than directly attacking) trying to find a weakness in the Union positions to their east. As the jockeying for an advantage continued, the Confederate troops launched all-out infantry assaults, marching by the thousands out of the woods and

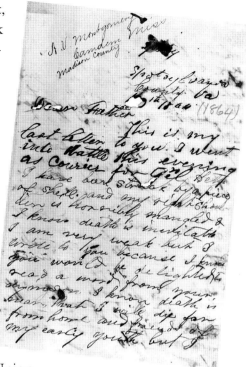

Mississippi private J. R. Montgomery's last letter to his father, stained with spots of blood from his battle wound at Spotsylvania, was painfully typical of letters written by soldiers on both sides from Gettysburg to Atlanta. ". . . I have been struck by a piece of shell . . . and I know death is inevitable," Montgomery wrote. ". . . My grave will be marked 58 that you may visit if you desire to do so. . . . Give my love to all my friends . . . my strength fails me. . . . May we meet in heaven."

THE 26TH NORTH CAROLINA TOOK 800 MEN INTO BATTLE AT GETTYSBURG AND SUFFERED 714 CASUALTIES.

across often open ground between their positions and the Union's fortified artillery locations. At one point a northern soldier remarked that the line of rebel soldiers moving forward looked to be a mile long. Union cannon and riflemen sent hundreds of thousands of rounds of grapeshot and bullets raining down on the southern troops. Soldiers fell on top of one another, dead or maimed, until the creeks nearly ran red with blood. More than fifty thousand men were injured or killed on the battlefields of Gettysburg.

Though Lee's army inflicted huge losses on the Union troops, his army suffered even more casualties. The South, but for a momentary breach of the northern lines, was stopped at every point. It was a major victory for the North. Lee's army was battered and turned back to the south, prevented completely from penetrating Union defenses. Lee's critical march north and east toward the largest cities in the Union was stopped completely and the tide had turned dramatically in favor of the North. It now had the decided advantage, yet it still took another two years to end the Civil War.

★ GETTYSBURG ADDRESS

This short speech has come to epitomize the Civil War for many people—students, teachers, and historians alike. Several months after the Battle of Gettysburg, President Lincoln was invited to offer "a few appropriate remarks" at the dedication of the national cemetery adjacent to the massive battlefield. The cemetery itself was a huge and hurried project to give a proper burial ground to those who had died just months earlier.

The ceremony's main speaker, orator Edward Everett, took nearly two hours to deliver his remarks; Lincoln spoke for only two minutes. Everett later commented that Lincoln did a better job giving meaning to the war in two short minutes than he had in two hours.

Historians often disagree on the meaning of significant events even when they agree on the facts. We will never know with absolute certainty how Lincoln viewed the address. No printed copies were given out to the press in advance of his speech and consequently it was often misquoted in newspapers.

Some accounts said the address was boring, while others felt Lincoln failed to address critical concerns as the war dragged on. Legend, not fact, says Lincoln jotted it down in minutes, on the train to Gettysburg. It would have been more typical of the president to ponder his words, no matter how brief, over the weeks prior to the event. He also supposedly voiced his own dissatisfaction either with his remarks or the crowd's reaction, immediately after delivering his address.

LINCOLN'S GETTYSBURG ADDRESS

Fourscore and seven years ago our fathers brought forth on this continent, a new nation, conceived in Liberty, and dedicated to the proposition that all men are created equal.

Now we are engaged in a great civil war, testing whether that nation, or any nation so conceived and so dedicated, can long endure. We are met on a great battle-field of that war. We have come to dedicate a portion of that field, as a final resting place for those who here gave their lives that that nation might live. It is altogether fitting and proper that we should do this.

But, in a larger sense, we can not dedicate—we can not consecrate—we can not hallow—this ground. The brave men, living and dead, who struggled here, have consecrated it, far above our poor power to add or detract. The world will little note, nor long remember what we say here, but it can never forget what they did here. It is for us the living, rather, to be dedicated here to the unfinished work which they who fought here have thus far so nobly advanced. It is rather for us to be here dedicated to the great task remaining before us—that from these honored dead we take increased devotion to that cause for which they gave the last full measure of devotion—that we here highly resolve that these dead shall not have died in vain—that this nation, under God, shall have a new birth of freedom—and that government of the people, by the people, for the people, shall not perish from the earth.

But one thing is indisputable: Lincoln said that "the world will little note, nor long remember what we say here, but it can never forget what they did here." It is ironic that just the opposite has taken place. Millions of people have recited Lincoln's words, yet a mere fraction of them know what the battle meant, how the soldiers fought, and how they died.

★ GRANT, ULYSSES S. (1822–1885)

U. S. Grant, recognizable as the face on the fifty-dollar bill, is also generally acknowledged as the foremost Union general. In 1911, on the fiftieth anniversary of the beginning of the war, a former officer who served under Grant said, "No more gentle-hearted and kindly man is known to American history, not excepting Abraham Lincoln."

Grant was not the quintessential general, nor even the typical soldier. He graduated from the U.S. Military Academy only twenty-first in his class of thirty-nine. Grant served as a captain in the Mexican War, but in 1854, he resigned his commission to enter private business. Unsuccessful as an entrepreneur, Grant returned to the military at the outbreak of the Civil War.

He said he deplored the misery and bloodshed of war; indeed, at a time when hunting was nearly a universal pastime, he refused to hunt for sport. Despite his many victories in the Civil War, many people questioned his military savvy and motives. One man who did not was his commander-in-chief, President Lincoln.

Lincoln sensed both the strength of Grant's convictions and his military insight, even if his unconventional tactics often ran counter to any military textbook. By 1862, Grant was a major general,

Ulysses S. Grant

and in March 1864, Lincoln gave him command of all the Union armies.

In July 1863, while George G. Meade was defeating the Confederate Army at Gettysburg, Grant was claiming victory at Vicksburg, Mississippi. He continued to hammer relentlessly at the fortified southern lines, and then for nearly a year kept Petersburg and Richmond, Virginia, under siege. Finally, Grant forced Lee into a position in which the Confederate general had no choice but to surrender.

Grant, riding the popularity he won as the war's victorious general, was elected president of the United States in the next two elections after the war, 1868 and 1872. The period known as Reconstruction was one of the most difficult, controversial, and scandalous in U.S. history. After leaving office in 1876—twelve years after the end of the Civil War, Grant once again proved unsuccessful in private business.

Author Mark Twain, an avid Grant supporter, encouraged the penniless and ill former president to write his memoirs. Twain would publish them and Grant, suffering from throat cancer, would be able to ensure that his family had an adequate income after his death. Grant's memoirs were well received throughout the country and became a huge financial success. His book is still regarded by both social and military historians as an outstanding Civil War history and military text.

With the war well into its third year, the goal of whomever wore this silk campaign ribbon was clearly both a Republican and a military victory.

★ GREELEY, HORACE (1811–1872)

Editor of the *New York Tribune*, Horace Greeley was one of the most influential newspapermen of the Civil War era. He challenged politicians before and during the war. He founded the *Tribune* in 1841 and was a strong abolitionist voice. He did not always support Lincoln but was a strong supporter of the war for several years. Greeley often frustrated politicians with his inconsistent views and

Horace Greeley

changes of opinions. In 1861, for example, when the Confederate Congress was about to take up official residence in Richmond, Virginia, Greeley urged Lincoln to move quickly to take the city. This hastened the Battle of Bull Run. Greeley then pushed for Lincoln to abandon the war effort completely and let the South have its independence. He was involved in a failed 1864 peace negotiation with the South in Niagara Falls, New York.

Greeley was a Republican and critical of the lenient treatment of the South after the war, but he also helped post bond money to free Jefferson Davis from prison. And it was Greeley who was so often quoted for his belief that the future of the country lay far beyond New York. He was forever linked to simple advice he reportedly offered, "Go West, Young Man."

TO SAVE THE UNION

So often, discussions simplify the Civil War into a battle over slavery. However, much of the disagreement that started the war was about the rights of the states to establish their own laws, even if they disagreed with federal laws that governed all citizens. When Horace Greeley chastised President Lincoln over the course of the war for not eradicating slavery, Lincoln responded plainly and concisely:

"My paramount object in this struggle is to save the Union, and is not either to save or destroy slavery. If I could save the Union without freeing any slave, I would do it; if I could save it by freeing all the slaves, I would do it; and if I could save it by freeing some and leaving others alone, I would also do that."

Lincoln has been known throughout history as "The Great Emancipator." Perhaps he would be equally or even more happy to be known as the man who saved the Union!

★ HAMLIN, HANNIBAL (1809–1891)

Lincoln's first vice president (1860–64), Hannibal Hamlin, was an early supporter of Lincoln in New England. While Hamlin believed that the government had no right to abolish slavery where it already existed, yet he also felt slavery should not be allowed to spread into new territories. Although Lincoln's platform was strongly antislavery and

Campaigning in 1860 was not unlike what we see today—posters, speeches, hand shaking, and even pins, tokens, and advertising.

THE 1ST MAINE HEAVY ARTILLERY IN A CHARGE AT PETERSBURG, VIRGINIA, IN JUNE 1864, LOST 635 OF ITS 900 MEN IN SEVEN MINUTES.

Hamlin's views tended to be closer to those of the Democrats, the Republican party hoped that the choice of Hamlin as a vice-presidential running mate would broaden Lincoln's appeal. In 1864, as the war dragged on, Hamlin was replaced by southern Democrat Andrew Johnson in an effort to win support. Johnson became president shortly after, when Lincoln was assassinated.

★ HAMPTON ROADS, VIRGINIA

On February 3, 1865, as the war neared its end, President Lincoln and Secretary of State William Seward met with three emissaries from Confederate President Jefferson Davis on a Union steamship at Hampton Roads, near the site of the battle between the *Monitor* and the *Merrimack*. The discussions were intended to be about terms of peace. Lincoln wanted to offer substantial assistance to the South, assuming the Confederacy was ready to stop fighting altogether. He suggested a payment of four hundred million dollars to compensate southern slaveowners for their slaves, a sum equal to about 15 percent of the pre-war value of all slaves in the South. Lincoln also suggested pardons, amnesty, and leniency for Confederate soldiers and leaders, but he would not waver on emancipation. President Davis, who despised Lincoln, called him "His Majesty Abraham the First." The South would fight on, Davis said, ignoring the fact that the Confederacy was nearly beaten already. With little meaningful opposition, Sherman's troops were marching their way through the South, burning and destroying virtually everything in their path. No longer was the question whether the Union would win the war, but how quickly the South would be forced to surrender and how much devastation it would suffer before then. If Davis had agreed to the terms of surrender offered at Hampton Roads, he could have saved huge portions of the countryside, homes, and cities he loved from destruction.

★ HANCOCK, WINFIELD SCOTT (1824–1886)

Winfield Scott Hancock was an experienced Union corps commander given the task of fortifying positions and holding them against the renewed Confederate efforts at Gettysburg. A Confederate victory at Gettysburg, on northern soil, might well have led to attacks on major northern cities and spurred the South to victory.

On the first day at Gettysburg, Hancock's men were positioned around Culp's and Cemetery hills, just south of the city of Gettysburg, in areas critical to the battle. When a fresh Alabama brigade of sixteen hundred charged Hancock's position, he dispatched a Minnesota regiment to repulse the attack. The 1st Minnesota, veterans numbering just three hundred men, fixed their bayonets and charged the oncoming soldiers. More than 80 percent of the Minnesota regiment were wounded or killed, but they

Union officers at Gettysburg pose for a photo in camp; later, all were wounded, and General Francis C. Barlow (standing at left) nearly died from his wounds.

successfully defended their position. On the second day at Gettysburg, Hancock commanded a portion of the Union Army assigned to defend Little Round Top, farther south of the city, to prevent it from being captured by the Confederate troops. For Hancock's bravery at Gettysburg and other Civil War battles, he won the nickname "Hancock the Superb."

★ HARPERS FERRY, VIRGINIA

A town at the junction of the Potomac and Shenandoah Rivers in Virginia, Harpers Ferry was the site of a vicious attack by John Brown, the zealous antislavery advocate. Brown believed God had chosen him to end slavery. His unprovoked attack on the federal armory at Harpers Ferry, in which his men killed several civilians and the town's mayor Fontaine Beckham, made the South more determined than ever to maintain slavery, despite the actions of passionate abolitionists. See *John Brown*.

Harpers Ferry, Virginia, a small town with little other significance during the Civil War, holds a critical place in history because of John Brown's attack.

★ HAY, JOHN (1838–1905)

An American statesman and writer, John Hay graduated from Brown University in 1858 and went on to study law in Springfield, Illinois. His friend John Nicolay introduced him to Abraham Lincoln. When Lincoln became president, Hay and Nicolay traveled to Washington as his private secretaries. Hay served in this position until Lincoln's death. Although only half Lincoln's age and somewhat carefree, Hay had enough confidence in his education and intelligence to be an honest and trusted critic of Lincoln's speeches and rhetoric. The two men often had long discussions about language and the use of words. Hay and Nicolay later wrote a critically acclaimed biography of Lincoln. Hay also served as secretary of state under presidents William McKinley and Theodore Roosevelt.

★ HERNDON, WILLIAM (1818–1891)

From 1844 until the president's death, William Herndon, known as "Billy," was Abraham Lincoln's partner in their Springfield, Illinois, law practice. Despite Lincoln's tenure in Washington, both in Congress and as president, he always considered Illinois his home and his law partnership his permanent business. In later years, Herndon wrote some of the earliest, firsthand accounts of the late president, and claimed to know him better than anyone else. He recalled that Lincoln had often brought his sons, Willie and Tad, into their office. Herndon would defer to Lincoln at the time and not complain, but he noted that although they "never disturbed the serenity of their father . . . many a time I wanted to wring the necks of those little brats and pitch them out of the windows!" See *Abraham Lincoln*.

An early ad placed by attorneys Lincoln and Herndon in the local Springfield, Illinois, newspaper.

AT LEAST SIXTY-THREE SEPARATE UNION REGIMENTS SUFFERED MORE THAN 50 PERCENT CASUALTIES IN SINGLE BATTLES.

★ HOLMES, OLIVER WENDELL, JR. (1841–1935)

Although not a hero in the Civil War, Oliver Wendell Holmes, Jr., was nevertheless a noteworthy participant, having been wounded three times and once left for dead on the battlefield. He enlisted in 1861 just before graduating from Harvard University, and he is said to have given President Lincoln, who was observing combat at the Battle of Fort Stevens, outside Washington, critical advice: "Get down," he yelled as the president observed the front line amid the spray of bullets. Mustered out as a captain when the war was over, Holmes returned to Harvard and became a lawyer in 1866. In 1909, the one-hundredth anniversary of Lincoln's birth, Holmes became a justice on the U.S. Supreme Court. He served almost thirty years and was one of the most famous and highly regarded judicial minds in the history of the high court.

★ HOOKER, JOSEPH (1814–1879)

Known as "Fighting Joe," Union General Joseph Hooker was a West Point graduate, an experienced veteran of the Mexican War, and a well-respected brigade commander during the first years of the Civil War. On the single bloodiest day of the war, at Antietam (Sharpsburg), Hooker rode a huge white horse so that his men could easily see him during battle. Of course, that meant the enemy could see him easily, as well. His Massachusetts Volunteers lost 224 of 334 men that day, and Hooker was shot through the foot.

Hooker had a reputation for talking and drinking too much, but his courage at Antietam earned him a reputation for leadership. In January 1863, Lincoln put him in command of the Union Army of the Potomac, though the president worried about Hooker's ambition and his cockiness. Hooker began planning a new campaign against the Confederate forces and announced, "May God have mercy on General Lee . . . for I shall have none." But

Hooker's command lasted for just one battle. In May, Hooker's troops met Lee's men at Chancellorsville, where the North lost seventeen thousand men in a devastating defeat. Lincoln removed Hooker from command and replaced him with General George Meade.

★ HOWE, JULIA WARD (1819–1910)

Julia Ward Howe was a poet and a staunch abolitionist. She believed the Union Army's mission was a holy one. After visiting the troops in Washington, DC, she was urged by a friend to provide better words for a tune the soldiers liked to sing. Howe came up with "The Battle Hymn of the Republic," which was first published in the *Atlantic Monthly* in 1862. Soon her words were being sung not only by soldiers while marching or relaxing around campfires, but by northern civilians as well. The Civil War was called by many a singing war; Howe's was perhaps its most famous song.

Throughout her life, Howe wrote and lectured. She worked for equal rights for women and founded, with Lucy Stone and others, the New England Women's Club, which later became the American Woman Suffrage Association. In 1907, she became the first woman elected to the American Academy of Arts and Letters.

J

★ JACKSON, THOMAS "STONEWALL" (1824–1863)

A master of military strategy, Confederate General Thomas Jackson always seemed to be everywhere the enemy thought he wasn't. He was one of Robert E. Lee's best, most cunning generals, continually surprising the Union forces with the skill and ferocity of his troops. Jackson earned his nickname for his bravery and refusal to pull back at the Battle of Bull Run (Manassas), where he was said to have stood like a stone wall. During and after the war, many people believed that the South could have won the bloody, decisive Battle of Gettysburg (and perhaps changed the entire fate of the nation) had Jackson been there. But Stonewall had died just two months earlier after being shot accidentally by his own men at the Battle of Chancellorsville. With several officers, he had been returning to his troops when some rebels mistook him for Union cavalry. Jackson took four bullets in his left arm. His arm was amputated, but he died of pneumonia eight days later. See *Battle of Chancellorsville, Virginia.*

★ JOHNSON, ANDREW (1808–1875)

When Lincoln ran for reelection in 1864, the Republican party selected Andrew Johnson, a Union Democrat and former senator and governor of Tennessee, as his vice-presidential running mate. Johnson was a strong supporter of the Union, but was not an antislavery moderate as was Lincoln. Johnson had worked his way up from poverty to become a wealthy landowner, politician—and for a while, slaveholder—so he understood the interests of southern whites who were not prosperous slaveowners. He supported the Union cause only because he hated the southern planter aristocracy.

After the assassination of President Lincoln, Johnson was sworn in as president and tried to follow Lincoln's policies for Reconstruction. On May 29, 1865, Johnson offered general amnesty for all Confederates who would take an oath of allegiance to the Union and support the emancipation of slaves. This allowed many who were powerful in the South before the war to regain their political power. Johnson also held fast to his dislike of Confederates, refusing to enforce many of the Reconstruction acts passed by the Republican Congress because they clashed with his policies. Fearing that his interference would prevent their plans from working, radical members of Congress tried to have him removed from office through impeachment, but Johnson was acquitted in the Senate by just a single vote. See *Reconstruction*.

Andrew Johnson

K

★ KANSAS-NEBRASKA ACT

Illinois Democratic Senator Stephen A. Douglas introduced the Kansas-Nebraska Act in the Senate in 1854. The act allowed the Kansas and Nebraska territories, which hoped to become states, to decide for themselves whether or not they would allow slavery. Douglas, a slaveowner years earlier, said that the residents of Kansas and Nebraska, not the federal government, should be allowed to determine whether the states would join the Union as free or slave. Douglas argued that passage of this act would encourage settlers to migrate west and that the ultimate decision whether or not to allow slavery in new states would then lie with voters in those states. The increased settlement would in turn necessitate building a transcontinental railway, which Douglas supported.

Many in the North were infuriated by the Kansas-Nebraska Act, which effectively displaced the Compromise of 1820. The controversy over the act and the growing tension between North and South spurred other changes. The Whig party crumbled, the Democrats (led by Douglas) were exerting far more power over Congress than many in the North could tolerate, and the new "anti-Nebraskan" or "Republican" party was formed. Its first

U.S. ARMY OFFICERS' RANKS

- General of the Army
- General
- Lieutenant General
- Major General
- Brigadier General
- Colonel
- Lieutenant Colonel
- Major
- Captain
- First Lieutenant
- Second Lieutenant

presidential candidate would be Abraham Lincoln in 1860. See *Compromise of 1850* and *Missouri Compromise.*

★ KENNESAW MOUNTAIN, BATTLE OF

As the war continued into 1864, the Union Army pressed deeper into the South. Sherman's March to the Sea, cutting a swath of devastation through what once had been thriving farms, cities, and plantations, hit a temporary bump in its journey—a battle on June 27, 1864, at Kennesaw Mountain, Georgia, twenty miles from Atlanta. By Civil War standards, the casualties were light: Sherman suffered two thousand, and the Confederates just a fourth of that total. More important to the Confederate Army, they had stopped the invading Union Army, even if only temporarily. The battle boosted the sagging morale of the southern troops, and the war dragged on for another year.

★ LEE, ROBERT E. (1807–1870)

Robert E. Lee was perhaps the most charismatic, gentlemanly, and talented of all the generals who fought on either side during the Civil War. To this day, he is revered throughout the South for his leadership and compassion. His father was Henry "Light Horse Harry" Lee, a hero during the Revolutionary War. Lee graduated second in his class from West Point and had served in the army for more than thirty years when the war began. Just prior to the war, he was sent to Harpers Ferry to put an end to John Brown's bloodshed. Like so many soldiers during the Civil War, Lee soon ended up fighting against former friends, classmates, and army regiment-mates.

Winfield Scott called Lee to Washington as war seemed imminent, but he couldn't entice the fifty-four-year-old colonel to stay with the U.S. Army. When Virginia seceded, so did Lee. He was not a staunch supporter of slavery, calling it both politically and morally wrong, but he believed strongly in states' rights. He had no desire to see the Union divided, but he was first and foremost a Virginian.

It was not long before he was in command of the Army of Northern Virginia, and a month later he became brigadier of the Confederacy, the highest Confederate army rank and one he held for the rest of the war. Until Gettysburg, Lee was remarkable in employing superior strategy and fewer troops to defeat the Union Army time after time. He won at Second Bull Run, fought the Union to a standoff at Antietam (a victory in itself), then defeated Burnside at Fredericksburg and Booker at Chancellorsville. He once said that the loss of so many of his generals in battle—especially Stonewall Jackson—ultimately cost him the war. After the war, he became president of Washington College, today known as Washington and Lee University in Virginia. He was as admired by his students as he was by his soldiers. He had been plagued with heart problems during the war and eventually died from heart disease in 1870 at age sixty-three.

Robert E. Lee

★ LIBBY PRISON

A converted, three-story chandlery (a place where candles are stored), Libby Prison in Richmond, Virginia, housed more than one thousand prisoners but was neither as gruesome—nor as escape-proof—as the South's infamous Andersonville Prison. In early 1864, more than one hundred prisoners tunneled under the basement and out into the streets of Richmond—almost as dangerous a place for Union soldiers to be as inside the prison! Eventually half were recaptured. One northern inmate, surrounded by doctors, lawyers, Europeans, farmers, ministers, and other prisoners, wrote that his best education on the human race had come from his confinement at Libby Prison.

A Union prisoner of war, literally a walking skeleton, is examined by a doctor after Libby Prison was liberated at the end of the war.

★ LINCOLN, ABRAHAM (1809–1865)

The sixteenth president of the United States, Abraham Lincoln was a keenly intelligent, articulate lawyer from a humble background. Perhaps the most unforgettable figure in American history, Lincoln was very tall and gangly, his hair never quite in place and his beard uneven. He looked plain and somewhat awkward, yet had a presence that easily won people's attention and respect. He was elected to Congress from Illinois in 1846, but did not seek reelection, instead returning to his law practice in Springfield, where he remained active in local politics.

Abraham Lincoln

The Kansas-Nebraska Act, however, so stirred Lincoln that he could not stay content in his hometown. He feared that slavery, rather than "dying a natural death" over time, would now spread throughout the territories and the entire nation. So in 1856 he joined the newly formed Republican party and returned to national politics. In 1858, he ran for the U.S. Senate against Stephen A. Douglas and lost, but a series of highly publicized debates throughout the state between the two men propelled Lincoln to national prominence. Few expected him to win the Republican nomination, but support continued to grow from the notoriety he earned from the debates. Lincoln's campaign was keenly focused, his message a persuasive call for the preservation of the Union. Still, he was considered the underdog until the Democratic party split between northern and southern factions. Lincoln won, becoming the first Republican president. Because the South saw him as opposed to slavery or at least as a president determined to make an anti-slavery stand, secession became a very real and immediate possibility. By the time Lincoln was inaugurated in March 1861, seven southern states had already seceded and formed the Confederate States of America. Lincoln's call for reconciliation between the North and South came too late.

The first shots fired by the Confederate troops in the Charleston, SC, harbor at Fort Sumter turned arguing and secession into war.

During his presidency, Lincoln aroused passionate feelings, both love and hate. Southerners felt he was destroying all they held dear, while Northerners dubbed him the "Great Emancipator." Lincoln's deepest concern was not for the plight of slaves, however, nor for the different cultures of the North and South, but for the survival of a country less than a century old with one of the finest democratic foundations ever conceived.

Deeply thoughtful, an incomparable writer with a gift for cutting to the heart of an issue in simple yet most powerful language, Lincoln never wavered in his belief that his oath of office required that he preserve the nation and its constitution. In all of his many writings, his most revered few words—the Gettysburg Address—offer a vivid window into the soul of a man fighting a war to save a country. At Gettysburg, Lincoln's few words addressed the pain and suffering of the tens of thousands of fathers, sons, brothers, and husbands whose bodies filled the graveyard and still lay strewn about the ground of the adjacent battlefield. His words— "that we here highly resolve that these dead shall not have died in vain . . . and that government of the people, by the people, for the people, shall not perish from the earth"— eloquently honored those

> "(DOUGLAS) HAS SET ABOUT SERIOUSLY TRYING TO MAKE THE IMPRESSION THAT WHEN WE MEET AT DIFFERENT PLACES I AM LITERALLY IN HIS CLUTCHES—THAT I AM A POOR, HELPLESS, DECREPIT MOUSE, AND THAT I CAN DO NOTHING AT ALL. . . . I DON'T WANT TO QUARREL WITH HIM—TO CALL HIM A LIAR—BUT WHEN I COME SQUARE UP TO HIM I DON'T KNOW WHAT ELSE TO CALL HIM."
>
> —*Abraham Lincoln*
> *From the fifth joint debate with Stephen Douglas,*
> *September 18, 1858, at Charleston*

who had died, but also painted a picture of the man who agonized over the suffering of the entire nation.

Lincoln lived to see the end of the Civil War, which came less than a month after his second inauguration. But before the country could even begin to mend itself, actor John Wilkes Booth, a southern extremist, assassinated Lincoln while he watched a play at Ford's Theatre not far from the U.S. Capitol. Lincoln was the first president to be killed in office.

★ LINCOLN, MARY TODD (1818–1882)

It was said that Abraham Lincoln never fell in love until he met Mary Todd, the short, plump, temperamental daughter of a wealthy Kentucky banker. The two seemed an unlikely couple: Abe a backwoods-born, rough-around-the-edges lawyer and Mary a well-educated member of the upper class. By Christmas 1840, Mary was engaged to Lincoln, though her family did not approve. Almost two years passed before they were married. Their first child, Robert Todd, was born in 1843, followed by Eddie in 1846, Willie in 1850, and Thomas (Tad) in 1853.

*Mary Todd
Lincoln*

Mary was interested in politics, and often spoke out about her views, an uncommon practice for a woman in the nineteenth century. She was very social and loved to entertain. She had difficulty coping with her role as the president's wife and was hurt by much of the public criticism she and her husband received.

Yet, as Lincoln's secretary of the navy, Gideon Welles, said, "Her face was an index to every passing emotion—without designing to wound she now and then indulged in sarcastic, witty remarks . . . but there was no malice in her."

The greatest joy in the Lincolns' lives were their children, and they lost two of them—Eddie in 1850 when he was not yet four years old, and Willie in 1862 at age twelve. Each death plunged the couple into deep depression, "too deep for the President or herself to refer to," Welles said. After her husband's murder in 1865 and son Tad's death in 1871, Mary never fully recovered. Her oldest son, Robert, eventually committed her to a mental institution. She died in 1882 at her sister's home.

★ LINCOLN-DOUGLAS DEBATES

Many people today, hearing of the debates, assume they were between Lincoln and Douglas as they competed for the presidency in 1860. In fact, they took place two years earlier, in 1858, as the two men—rivals in their home state of Illinois for some twenty years—met to debate, slavery the selected topic. Douglas won that election, but Lincoln emerged as a new, strong personality in national politics.

In the debates, Lincoln pointed out that he and the Republicans cared about the spread of slavery in territories and new states and the northern Democrats did not. Douglas did not say that Democrats were pro-slavery, but that they were neutral. That position eventually cost him votes in the presidential election of 1860, as the southern Democrats voted for their own strongly pro-slavery candidate. But in 1858, the debates between the starkly different men—in appearance and in politics—drew national attention to Illinois. Amazingly, as the men traveled throughout Illinois and argued the issues, the crowds were immense for that era: fifteen thousand one night, twenty thousand the next.

Men walked through the debate crowds selling campaign buttons and

"I WILL SAY HERE, WHILE UPON THIS SUBJECT, THAT I HAVE NO PURPOSE, DIRECTLY OR INDIRECTLY, TO INTERFERE WITH THE INSTITUTION OF SLAVERY IN THE STATES WHERE IT EXISTS. I BELIEVE I HAVE NO LAWFUL RIGHT TO DO SO, AND I HAVE NO INCLINATION TO DO SO."

—*Abraham Lincoln*
From the first joint debate,
August 21, 1858, Ottawa

The seven Lincoln-Douglas debates drew huge crowds—as many as twenty thousand—as the people were hungry for strong leadership. The 1858 election had national political writers closely watching the outcome.

ribbons. Reporters took notes and rushed telegraphed reports to their papers. Boston and Atlanta residents knew what Lincoln and Douglas had said the day before. Douglas, just five feet four inches tall, was the slick politician whose voice filled the air across the crowd. The nation *could* endure half slave and half free, he said. Lincoln said it could not.

Senate elections were settled in the legislature then, not by popular vote. The Democrats won the state legislature by a slim margin, sending Douglas, the incumbent, back to Washington.

Despite Douglas's dramatic advantage in political savvy, the nation had heard what Lincoln said and liked it. He was soon talked about as a presidential candidate in 1860. He was honest, sincere, articulate, and would not be trapped into saying what he didn't mean. It was a vibrant, exciting series of debates, and it vaulted Lincoln toward the presidency.

★ LIVERMORE, MARY (1820–1905)

The U.S. Sanitary Commission was formed early in the war to collect and distribute to soldiers everything from food, clothing, bandages, and medicine to paper, ink, and pens. One of the thousands of women volunteers had an even more ambitious idea: to create a fund-raising fair where common citizens, businessmen, and politicians could provide even more for the soldiers. Commission managers laughed at Mary Livermore when she said she would raise twenty-five thousand dollars for the troops, but the Chicago Sanitary Fair she organized was a huge success. She continued organizing fairs throughout the country, which resulted in hundreds of thousands of dollars' worth of goods being donated, goods that were auctioned to raise money to purchase supplies, clothing, food, and more for Union soldiers. Even President Lincoln participated, donating his autograph to be auctioned at one of the fairs. See *U.S. Sanitary Commission*.

Mary Livermore

★ LONGSTREET, JAMES (1821–1904)

The Battle of the Wilderness in May 1864 took the lives of two Union generals, James Wadsworth and John Sedgwick. Confederate General James Longstreet nearly died, too, when he was hit by gunfire from his own troops. Severely wounded, he was back in the saddle five months later. Forty years old when the war began, Longstreet had already been badly wounded during the Mexican War. Longstreet commanded troops at Gettysburg, where he disagreed with Robert E. Lee's decision to mount a massive frontal attack. After the war, Longstreet settled in New Orleans, became friends with Ulysses Grant, became a Republican, and also served as minister to Turkey and as a Railroad Commissioner. Many Southerners criticized him for becoming a Republican and befriending Grant, but he ignored them and took pleasure in outliving most of those who disapproved of his postwar politics.

★ LUCIFERS

The wooden stick matches that soldiers used came in strips of ten to twenty that could easily be pulled off one at a time as needed. Soldiers referred to these invaluable matches as "Lucifers" (the devil) and usually kept them in "match safes"—small, often engraved, metal flip-top boxes. The matches were more valuable than money in the field—the difference between light and dark, cold meals or hot.

Union troops from the 5th New Hampshire and 64th New York build a bridge over the Chickahominy River as part of General McClellan's efforts to advance toward the Confederate capital of Richmond, Virginia.

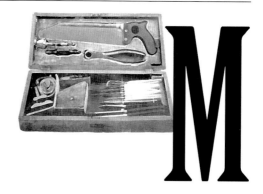

M

★ MANASSAS

See *Battle of Bull Run*.

★ McCLELLAN, GEORGE BRINTON (1826–1885)

Many soldiers came out of retirement when the Civil War began, especially older officers whose experience and leadership were needed. George McClellan left the military in 1857 and became vice president of the Illinois Central Railroad. In 1861, a retired veteran though only thirty-five years of age, he returned to the army and was given the rank of major general. McClellan successfully organized thousands of raw recruits into the new, powerful Army of the Potomac. His troops liked and respected him, affectionately calling him "Little Mac." He quickly fell into disfavor with Lincoln and his advisers, however, who disapproved of his fighting methods. McClellan often overestimated the strength of enemy troops and on several occasions hesitated or failed to attack, which Lincoln saw as a weakness. Lincoln blamed McClellan for the South's repeated and unexpected defeats of the larger Union forces. Lincoln replaced McClellan with Ambrose Burnside in November 1862. McClellan resigned from the army a second time and ran for president against Lincoln in 1864, an election many felt Lincoln might lose because the war had dragged on much longer than anyone expected. But Lincoln's popularity remained (the strongest among the U.S. troops), and his political victory was followed by the eventual military victory the following year.

★ MCPHERSON, JAMES BIRDSEYE (1828–1864)

When the war broke out, James McPherson was an engineer teaching at the military academy at West Point. He was instrumental in the outcome in the battles of Corinth and Vicksburg and was given command of the Union's Army of the Tennessee (succeeding Sherman) in early 1864. In July of that year, surveying the wooded area outside Atlanta with Sherman, he heard gunfire between Union and Confederate troops nearby. He told Sherman that he had attended West Point with their opponent, General John Hood. A mediocre student, McPherson said, he had become a formidable leader and should be respected. McPherson quickly sent riders to assemble troops and protect a critical hillside overlooking Atlanta. After discuss-

A group of Union Army surgeons pose in a rare moment of calm, their uniforms uncharacteristically clean. In performing amputations, many surgeons feared that anesthetics were too dangerous for patients. Some used chloroform, which put a patient to sleep as he inhaled it, but many provided only a sip of whiskey and a strong man to hold the patient down.

ing strategy with Sherman, McPherson rode to another position in the Union lines, where Confederate troops confronted him. When they ordered him to surrender, he wheeled his horse around to escape and was shot to death. The loss of McPherson at just thirty-six years of age was significant. He was one of Grant's favorite combat officers, second only to Sherman.

★ MEADE, GEORGE GORDON (1815–1872)

When Lincoln selected George Meade to replace Joseph Hooker as wartime commander of the Army of the Potomac, he knew Lee's army was heading to Pennsylvania, Meade's home. Lincoln thought the general would fight at his best defending his own soil. Lincoln was right, and during the Battle of Gettysburg, Meade was zealous and successful. He went on to command the Union troops at other important battles, including the Wilderness and Petersburg.

★ MEDICAL CARE

Disease was the greatest killer during the Civil War. Though bullets, bayonets, cannon, and grapeshot killed a staggering numbering of men—six hundred thousand—for every soldier killed on the battlefield, two more succumbed to scurvy, dysentery, typhoid, diphtheria, pneumonia, or other illnesses.

The Civil War field medical kit typically contained a saw for amputations and a plierlike tool to extract bullets, both of which can be seen in the lid section of the case.

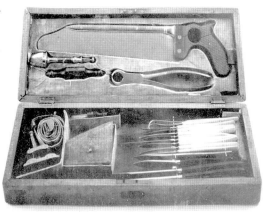

Surgeons and would-be surgeons did their best under battlefield conditions too terrible to imagine. Hospital-tent floors ran thick with blood and flesh; outside, ambulances and wagons were emptied as fast as doctors could amputate torn limbs. Piles of arms and legs several feet high were a common sight near a surgeon's tent.

Amputations were often done with

Injured soldiers' chances for recovery increased dramatically if they lived long enough to be moved from a field hospital tent to a real hospital in the city. These Union soldiers are recovering at the Armory Square General Hospital in Washington, DC.

no anesthetic; hygiene was nonexistent. So many wounds were caused by big, soft lead bullets shot at short distances that mangled bones were a typical by-product of gunshot injuries. Battlefield hospitals spread disease and infection; city hospitals were cleaner, better lit, and much more comfortable for the wounded soldier lucky enough to make it back to one. Still, often that only meant delaying death for a few days.

In prison, disease was even more prevalent. Virtually everyone had dysentery; there was no sanitation, and scurvy,

Dressed in exotic Zouave uniforms, several soldiers pretend to be wounded while their comrades practice an ambulance drill. In a true battle, this scene would not have been so peaceful or organized. Ambulance workers often had to dodge bullets to reach their patients.

measles, and infection killed tens of thousands of men on both sides.

⭐ MINIÉ, CLAUDE/MINIÉ BALL

The "minié" ball, a new type of bullet, was one of the most important innovations in Civil War weaponry. Often misspelled as "mini," the name had nothing to do with the bullet's size, but rather with its inventor, French Captain Claude Minié. Before the Civil War, the musket ball was the ammunition of choice. It was difficult to load, however, and often required extensive hammering to ram it down a rifle's barrel. The smaller minié ball could be pushed down easily. Because its hollow base expanded when fired, miniés gripped the inside of the barrel and spun, resulting in a straighter and longer flight. American James H. Burton refined the minié ball's design, making a cheaper version that was used extensively during the Civil War. The inch-long minié ball—millions of which were fired during the war—was accurate at 250 yards, five times the distance of musket-ball weapons.

⭐ MISSOURI COMPROMISE

In 1818, the Missouri Territory applied to become the twenty-third state in the Union. The region's settlers

Approximately two hundred thousand black men served in the Union Army, but they were segregated and treated as second-class soldiers, receiving less pay and fewer provisions than white recruits. The Union Navy, however, had difficulty filling its ranks and was more eager to enlist black men. It recruited twenty thousand black volunteers, and the limited space on ships made it impractical to separate black and white sailors. The men worked, ate, slept, and fought alongside one another, regardless of race.

wanted Missouri to be admitted as a slave state, but this was widely opposed in the North. At that time, there were eleven states in the North and eleven in the plantation-rich South. Admitting Missouri as a slave state would alter the balance of power and would affect congressional voting and the political direction of the country for many years to come.

Henry Clay, senator from Kentucky, came forward with a solution to deadlocked legislation. Under the new agreement, known as the Missouri Compromise, the new state of Missouri would be allowed to enact a state constitution that did not restrict slavery, while the far northern (and certainly free) state of Maine would be added, preserving the balance of power between the northern (free) and southern (slave) states. The Compromise outlawed slavery in all remaining territories of the Louisiana Purchase north of the southern boundary of Missouri.

★ MONITOR AND MERRIMACK

The most famous, although perhaps not the most significant, naval battle of the Civil War was between the U.S. *Monitor* and the Confederate *Merrimack,* two ironclad vessels. The Confederate Navy began converting a former frigate, the *Merrimack,* into an ironclad warship in 1861. When the Union Navy discovered the work was under way on the *Merrimack,* they rushed to build their own ironclad vessel, hiring John Ericsson as the engineer. The smaller *Monitor* was easier to maneuver and had a large rotating turret in the center with only two guns, compared with the *Merrimack*'s five on each side. When renovations on the *Merrimack* were completed, it was renamed the *Virginia,* and it began destroying Union ships at Hampton Roads, Virginia. The Union Navy sent the *Monitor* to defend its ships. The two ironclads met on March 9, 1862, and after four and a half hours of cannonballs bouncing off their protec-

tive metal sides, neither ship was able to sink or even significantly damage the other. No men were killed, and only two minor injuries were reported. The battle was a draw.

It was the first naval battle between iron ships, and it dramatically changed naval warfare from that point forward. The wooden warships that had dominated the oceans of the world were suddenly considered out-of-date. The English (with the most powerful navy in the world) announced they had only two worthy fighting ships—two ironclads—and the rest were obsolete. Worldwide, every navy began armor-plating its warships and hurrying to build new ones.

*The ironclad above was known as the **Merrimack** in the North, the **Virginia** in the South. It was the first American ironclad, and soon met its nemesis in the Union's **Monitor**. The **Merrimack** was massive compared to the **Monitor**, but their famous battle was a standoff. Even as a draw, the battle was a victory for the North, as the damaged **Merrimack** was unable to continue its attacks on Union shipping.*

★ MOSBY, JOHN SINGLETON (1833–1916)

In the South, the Partisan Ranger Act of 1862 allowed nonsoldiers to serve the Confederacy in organized units that attacked men, property, and arms of the enemy. They then sold whatever they took to the Confederate government. Far and away the boldest and most famous of these Confederate pseudosoldiers was John Singleton Mosby, known as the "Gray Ghost" for his stealth and daring. Mosby was highly appreciated for all he brought to the southern army. Lee acknowledged him as one of the most valuable of his wartime "officers."

Mosby was practicing law when the war began. During the Civil War, he organized a group of eight hundred partisan rangers who worked in groups of twenty to eighty to destroy rail lines and bridges, attack Union outposts and supply trains, and steal Union property. The Union Army despised Mosby and his guerrilla tactics, but they could not stop him from stealing their weapons and supplies. George Custer captured and executed six of Mosby's men in 1864; Mosby retaliated by killing seven of Custer's soldiers. On one occasion, a frustrated General Philip Sheridan reportedly sent one hundred soldiers to hunt down and kill or capture Mosby and his men. All but two of the Union men were wounded or killed, and the weapons of the dead ended up in the hands of Confederate troops. Mosby, wounded seven times during the war but never captured, was still successfully robbing supply trains and ambushing Union troops when the war ended.

Northern munitions and ordnance were vastly superior to those of the South. This staging area distributed weaponry to Union armies.

★ NEWSPAPERS

The newspapers of the Civil War were the link throughout the entire North and to a lesser degree in the South. *Frank Leslie's Illustrated* and *Harper's Weekly* had reporters and sketch artists in the field, literally following troops into battle. From New York to Atlanta, major city (and small town) dailies and weeklies brought remarkably accurate news to the general population, and they did it quickly. Mothers and fathers, husbands and sons could read in great detail how their men fared against the enemy just a few days earlier, a thousand miles away.

This Vicksburg, Mississippi, paper looks normal, but it was just a single sheet, the front filled with as much news as editors could squeeze in, and the back the floral design of the wallpaper on which it was printed; the design in the background of the photo is the actual wallpaper on which the **Vicksburg Sentinel** *is printed.*

BY THE NUMBERS

The following numbers include 1860 census figures on population, men in the military from war data, and deaths from post–Civil War government figures.

- *Northern Population: 22.3 million*

- *Southern Population: 9.1 million (5.6 million white and 3.5 million slaves)*

- *Number of Men in the Union Military Service: 2.2 million*

- *Number of Men in the Confederate Military Service: 1.4 million*

- *Number of Black Soldiers Serving in Union Army: 180,000*

- *Union Soldiers in Confederate Prisons: 200,000*

- *Union Deaths in Confederate Prisons: 30,000*

- *Confederate Soldiers in Union Prisons: 215,000*

- *Confederate Deaths in Union Prisons: 26,000*

Union artillery masses for the beginning of a march toward Confederate positions. With its gun carriages, heavy cannon, horse teams, and loads of ammunition, the artillery was the most time-consuming branch of the army to assemble before battle. Artillery soldiers in many cases were far enough behind the action that their casualties were lower, but they inflicted massive damage.

Even spies studied the papers to ensure they had correct information on troop movements. As the war dragged on, every aspect of daily life in the South became more difficult. Food, clothing, military supplies, and raw materials were difficult to come by in the South but still plentiful in the North. And the South's money was so inflated that when supplies could be found they were often too expensive. The papers reported it, and soon they fell victim to it. The South could not maintain its production of paper, either, and newspapers ceased publication. At one point, a handful of small southern papers continued to survive, not thrive, printing sparse bits of news on the backs of wallpaper.

★ NICOLAY, JOHN G. (1832–1901)

Like John Hay, John Nicolay was a private secretary to Abraham Lincoln during his presidency. Nicolay worked many years on the impressive ten-volume biography of Lincoln, which he coauthored with Hay and which remains a highly regarded and insightful look at the president. See *John Hay*.

P

★ PETERSBURG, VIRGINIA

At Petersburg and neighboring Richmond, the capital of the Confederacy, Lee and Grant faced off in 1864 and 1865 in a nearly year-long battle of bloody chess. When Grant marched more than one hundred thousand men to meet the entrenched Confederates, he lost two men to every one Lee lost; but the North gained a decided advantage because it had reinforcements, while the South continued to see its manpower and supplies dwindle with every passing day.

Grant discovered he could not break through Lee's positions with frontal attacks, but he was determined to lay siege to Petersburg and Richmond, hammering away at the undermanned but well-defended Confederate Army. At one point while Petersburg was under seige, Union forces built a nearly half-mile-long pontoon bridge in eight hours, crossed it, and then took two days to march around Lee. In an effort to surprise the Confederate troops, Army engineers also laid new railroad track south from Washington to resupply the Union Army while Lee's troops suffered through months of dangerously low stores of food, medical supplies, and ammunition.

The siege at Petersburg often included more creativity

than success for the North. One time, the Union Army tunneled literally to the Confederates' doorstep and then filled the underground cavern with explosives. The ensuing blast scared both sides, and the Union troops lost their advantage when they failed to attack quickly. The Union troops, finally moving forward, were gunned down in the crater left by the explosion. Later, an attempt to build a five-hundred-foot-long canal to join two waterways was also a failure. Eventually, the well-supplied and reinforced Union troops pushed through amid cannon fire and brought the inevitable evacuation of both Petersburg and the southern capital.

Black combat troops played a major role in the seige, and eventual defeat, of Petersburg. When the city was finally taken, they were among the first to march into the nearly abandoned city, greeted by now-freed slaves that came out to meet them.

★ PICKETT, GEORGE EDWARD (1825–1875)

Like so many Civil War officers, George Pickett was a veteran of the Mexican War. He also served in the Wash-

3,530 INDIANS FOUGHT FOR THE UNION, SUFFERING ALMOST 30 PERCENT CASUALTIES OR MORE THAN 1,000 DEAD AND WOUNDED.

ington Territory prior to the Civil War. When the war began, he resigned, taking a position as colonel in the Confederate Army. The following year he was made brigadier general. He led, at Robert E. Lee's behest under General Longstreet's reluctant orders, an ill-advised assault, known as Pickett's Charge, on Cemetery Hill at Gettysburg. It has always been considered one of the most infamous moments of that tumultuous three-day battle. In one-half hour, he lost approximately two-thirds of his men and was unable to break through the Union's fortified position. Pickett was later defeated at Lynchburg and was part of the surrender of the Army of Northern Virginia. After the war, he was offered military posts, but he never overcame the depression caused by his disastrous charge at Gettysburg. He lived in Richmond after the war and died in 1875.

★ PICKETT'S CHARGE

If Gettysburg was a turning point in the war, then Pickett's Charge was a pivotal point in that terrible battle. The Union established fortified positions on hills and rocky outcroppings, while the Confederates massed along the tree lines. "The Confederate columns must have been a mile long," one entrenched Union soldier said as the southern troops marched toward northern positions. Southern General George Pickett marched his men out of the woods and toward Cemetery Hill, where they were gunned down by Union rifles and artillery. Fighting was face-to-face, gun-to-gun, and head-to-head. Nothing seemed to stop the determined Confederate troops as they marched over and around their wounded and dead. The Union defensive position broke only briefly in one place, known as the Angle, where General Lewis A. Armistead of North Carolina actually leaped the wall and seized a Union gun battery, only to be shot seconds later. Dying, Armistead asked

Union General Winfield Scott Hancock to contact his family. Armistead and Hancock had been good friends before the war. Northern artillerymen said that the Confederates were so thickly stretched across the open ground that it was impossible to shoot and not hit someone.

Pickett never forgave Lee for "sending him to slaughter." The South had fifteen regimental commanders at Gettysburg; every one of them was wounded or killed, along with three generals and eight colonels. In one company, the University Greys, students from the University of Mississippi, every man in the unit was either wounded or killed in the charge. The Union lines held, and Lee's troops turned back to the south.

Hastily created cemeteries, often filled with unmarked graves, could be seen across the United and Confederate States everywhere there was a battle or even just a small skirmish.

★ POPE, JOHN (1822–1892)

It was said that only one officer of the Union Army earned the personal ire of Robert E. Lee. John Pope alienated his subordinates, his men, and Lee, among others. Lee was one of many Southerners who hated Pope's harsh treatment of civilians. Pope encouraged looting of southern homes and farms and threatened to kill any civilians suspected of aiding Confederate soldiers. On one occasion, he openly criticized new men under his command for their efforts in the East, while touting those under his former command in the West. Soundly defeated during Second Bull Run, he quickly blamed subordinates for the defeat. When Lincoln consolidated armies, McClellan took what had been Pope's troops, and the controversial general spent nearly three years of the war dealing with Sioux Indian problems instead of the Confederate Army.

★ PRISONS

See *Andersonville, Belle Isle,* and *Libby.*

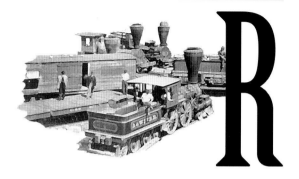

R

★ RECONSTRUCTION

The first decade after the end of the war was known as Reconstruction, because the entire nation—particularly the South—had to be "reconstructed" after the social, political, and geographic ravages of war. The federal government, and local and state governments primarily in the South, faced the overwhelming task of integrating freed slaves into daily life and rebuilding the southern economy

The first black men to serve in Congress following the Civil War: seated from left, Hiram R. Revels, senator from Mississippi, and Representatives Benjamin S. Turner (Alabama), Josiah T. Walls (Florida), Joseph H. Rainey (South Carolina), and Robert Brown Elliott (South Carolina). Standing from left, Representatives Robert C. De Large (South Carolina) and Jefferson F. Long (Georgia).

Many Civil War newspapers continued to thrive during postwar Reconstruction. **Harper's Weekly,** *which called itself "a Journal of Civilization," devoted hundreds of pages to the plight of freed slaves during Reconstruction.*

that had been so heavily based on slavery and plantations. Reconstruction brought with it free, and not always honest, elections. Some blacks voted and some were elected to public office. But corruption was widespread, and freedom did not necessarily mean happiness or opportunity. Freed blacks arriving in the North found widespread prejudice, a lack of jobs, and day-to-day life a challenge just to survive. In the South, the problems were much worse. Violence, hatred, and racism lasted long after the war ended. In fact, it was nearly a full century after slavery was abolished before the federal government would guarantee that blacks could sit next to whites on buses, eat next to whites at lunch counters, and go to school next to whites in the same classrooms.

★ THE REPUBLICAN PARTY

Abraham Lincoln was the first Republican president. The party grew out of the Democrats' longtime rival, the Whig party, which faded as the Republican party emerged. Lincoln had been a Whig congressman. The Whigs believed in a strong central government, as did the new Republican party. The new party grew out of dissatisfaction with the condition of the country and the deterioration of relations between the North and the South. As Lincoln called for strong adherence to the Constitution, the Democratic party began to split down geographic lines. Northern Democrats selected one candidate, southern Democrats another, and the three-way election gave Lincoln the victory in 1860. In 1864, Andrew Johnson, a former Democrat, ran as Lincoln's vice-presidential candidate and thus became president when Lincoln was assassinated. Johnson actually maintained many of the Reconstruction plans outlined by Lincoln and the Republican party. The Republicans wanted a strong national government while still protecting all individuals' constitutional rights. When the southern states rejoined the Union, many states' rights supporters and former slaveowners were elected to Congress, keeping many prewar arguments alive despite the end of slavery.

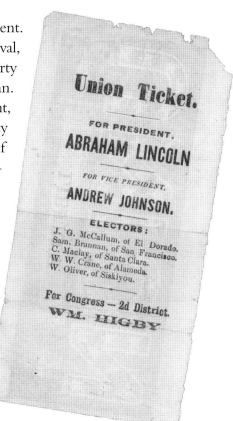

This paper handbill is much like you might see today—the Republican candidates for president and the local congressional candidate from California.

Richmond, capital of the Confederacy, was virtually destroyed by the war, while just over a hundred miles north, Washington, DC, was unscathed.

★ RICHMOND, VIRGINIA

The capital of the Confederacy, Richmond was little more than a hundred miles south of Washington, DC, the capital of the Union. As Union troops approached Richmond near the end of the war, rebel soldiers evacuated the city, setting much of it on fire to keep valuable supplies from falling into the hands of their enemy. On April 3, 1865, Union officers finally lowered the Confederate flag on the capitol building in Richmond, signaling the imminent defeat of the South. President Lincoln, with his son Tad at his side, visited the fallen city the next day. Six days later, General Robert E. Lee, commander of the Confederate Army, surrendered at Appomattox Court House in Virginia.

★ Scott, Dred (ca. 1800–1858)

A slave and personal servant to John Emerson, a U.S. army surgeon, Dred Scott became an important part of U.S. history because of an 1857 Supreme Court decision. Emerson took Scott with him wherever the army sent him, throughout the free states of Illinois and Wisconsin, and ultimately into the slave state of Missouri. When Emerson died in Missouri, Scott sued for his freedom on the grounds that he had traveled through and lived in free territory with Emerson for years before moving to Missouri. Supreme Court Chief Justice Roger Taney did not just rule on the case before him, but instead handed down a constitutional law opinion with implications far outside of what was being tried. He ruled that blacks, whether slave or free, could not sue in federal court because they were not citizens according to the Constitution. Further, he said that it did not matter where a slave lived: A slave could not be deemed free just for having lived in a free state. Taney wrote that the nation's founders had regarded slaves "as beings of an inferior order and altogether unfit to associate with the white race . . . so far inferior that they had no rights which a white man was bound to respect." Outrage over the Dred Scott decision further divided the country on the issues

THE UNION ARMY EXECUTED 267 SOLDIERS, SUFFERED 391 KNOWN SUICIDES, 520 MURDERS, AND 4,144 ACCIDENTAL DEATHS.

of states' rights and slavery, the two major issues that led to the war four years later. The ruling obviously enraged those in the abolitionist movement and stalled temporarily their progress. It also was one more factor in widening the North-South gap leading to what many felt was inevitable war. See *Roger B. Taney.*

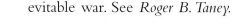

SECESSION

On March 4, 1861, Abraham Lincoln became the sixteenth president of the United States; two weeks earlier, on February 18, Jefferson Davis had been sworn in as the president of the newly formed Confederate States of America, which stretched from South Carolina to Texas. The press in the southern states said that the election of Lincoln was like a declaration of war, noting that the "South will never submit to such humiliation and degradation as the inauguration of Abraham Lincoln" and what they perceived as his desire to free southern slaves.

Secession had more to do with northern economic dominance over the plantation-based economy of the South and federal versus states' rights than slavery. But slavery became the heated focal point as secession became reality. Once the outcome of the election of 1860 was known, the move toward secession and the formation of an independent southern nation progressed quickly. The government and military leaders of the Confederate states were the congressmen, West Point graduates, friends, and colleagues of those in the North. Once the new government was in place and the first shots were fired, both sides buried the thought that they were all Americans. They now were two very different countries at war with one another over a way of life neither felt they could give up.

Union government leaders spent a great deal of time claiming that the southern states did not have the right to secede or to establish a separate government. Regardless,

CHARLESTON
MERCURY

EXTRA:

Passed unanimously at 1.15 o'clock, P. M., December 20th, 1860.

AN ORDINANCE

To dissolve the Union between the State of South Carolina and other States united with her under the compact entitled " The Constitution of the United States of America."

We, the People of the State of South Carolina, in Convention assembled, do declare and ordain, and it is hereby declared and ordained,

That the Ordinance adopted by us in Convention, on the twenty-third day of May, in the year of our Lord one thousand seven hundred and eighty-eight, whereby the Constitution of the United States of America was ratified, and also, all Acts and parts of Acts of the General Assembly of this State, ratifying amendments of the said Constitution, are hereby repealed; and that the union now subsisting between South Carolina and other States, under the name of " The United States of America," is hereby dissolved.

THE

UNION
IS
DISSOLVED!

On December 20, 1860, 169 South Carolina delegates met in a state convention to vote on secession: The vote was unanimous to secede and within minutes the **Charleston Mercury** *published a special edition announcing the vote.*

Regardless of the battle, the drummer boys signaled the infantry march with what was known as the "long roll." In a war where three generations might be fighting in the same army, there were teens on the front lines and younger boys still as regimental mascots beating the drum . . . and occasionally picking up a gun and firing at the enemy.

they did and the two halves of this country were engaged in a war Lincoln said would determine if the nation "could long endure." Lincoln has been studied and analyzed more than any president, and it was his emotional concern for the salvation of the country that led him to battle so heroically to defeat secession and reunite the country. But for all the political discussions about legality or constitutionality, the results were indisputable: Six hundred thousand Americans died in four years in a civil war, countless homes and lives were ruined, massive portions of the country were destroyed, and slavery was finally abolished. When the South surrendered, it agreed to dissolve its country and reenter the United States under the terms granted by the victorious North.

★ THE SEVEN DAYS' BATTLES

When Confederate commander Joseph E. Johnston was severely wounded in a battle near Richmond in May 1862, Robert E. Lee took over his command. Lee renamed his troops the Army of Northern Virginia and was put in charge of defending Richmond, the capital of the Confederacy. Union General George B. McClellan was advancing from the east in an attempt to capture Richmond. Lee sent his cavalry chief, Jeb Stuart, on a reconnaissance mission leading twelve hundred troops on a three-day, 150-mile ride around McClellan's army to gain information on its strength and position. As McClellan's army approached Richmond, Lee attacked, starting the first of five battles that lasted for seven days. Many of the casualties—nearly fifteen hundred men—were carried into Richmond, where "every house was open for the wounded," according to local residents. McClellan actually won four of five battles, but continued backing away from Lee's army despite his victories. In the Seven Days' Battles, Lee had driven McClellan back from Richmond and demonstrated his capabilities as a commander—capabilities that would be seen time and time again in the coming years of the war.

★ SEWARD, WILLIAM (1801–1872)

William Seward, lawyer, abolitionist, and former governor of New York, was a leader of the Whig party and a candidate for president in 1860. He chose to leave the fading Whigs and join the Republican party. After losing the presidential nomination, Seward vigorously supported Lincoln. He was rewarded with the cabinet position of secretary of state. Seward took the position, assuming he could dominate the less-experienced Lincoln and further his own political goals. He soon realized, as many did, that he had greatly underestimated the skill, intelligence, and strength of Lincoln. Seward found his niche handling foreign affairs rather than involving himself in day-to-day war decisions. On the night Lincoln was assassinated, one of the conspirators attacked Seward as well. He was stabbed while in his bed recovering from a carriage accident. He stayed on to serve Andrew Johnson and was responsible for "Seward's Folly," the 1867 purchase of Alaska from Russia that many Americans ridiculed as a pointless waste of money, never guessing the future military (because of its location during World War II, for example) and economic value the forty-ninth state would bring to the country. He retired from public life when Grant assumed the presidency.

★ SHARPSBURG

See *Battle of Antietam*.

Black soldiers were not immediately or universally accepted by their fellow Union troops. They fought bravely (twenty-five black Union soldiers and sailors earned the Congressional Medal of Honor) in battle, and fought long months and years for equality even in military service. Among other disparities, their pay was not equal to that of white soldiers.

★ SHAW, ROBERT GOULD (1837–1863)

Colonel Robert Gould Shaw was only twenty-six years old when he was killed in 1863 leading the 54th Massachusetts into battle at Battery Wagner on Morris Island, South Carolina. The son of a prominent Boston abolitionist family, Shaw was promoted to colonel and given the task of forming the first black regiment in the North.

His troops performed with dedication and valor attacking the Confederate battery. Their position was terrible. They had to charge across open, sandy ground to reach the fort. Their assault failed, and one-quarter of the regiment were killed, including Shaw. The Confederates were so angered to see a white man leading black troops that they dumped Shaw's body into a common grave with his men, intending to insult him. Shaw's parents responded differently, however. They thought that it was an honor for their son to have been buried with "his brave, devoted followers." While nearly two hundred thousand black troops served during the war, many in combat, the 54th gained notoriety as much for being the first to prove black soldiers could fight well as for the fight itself.

★ SHERIDAN, PHILIP HENRY (1831–1888)

Just five feet four inches tall and weighing less than 120 pounds, Philip Henry Sheridan was a smaller-than-average man. But he was one of the North's most famous generals and most skilled cavalry soldiers. Lincoln told Sheridan, "When this particular war began, I thought a cavalryman should be at least six feet four inches high, but I have changed my mind. Five feet four will do . . ." Sheridan distinguished himself at the battles of Chickamauga and Chattanooga and was placed in command of the Army of the Potomac. In August 1864, Ulysses Grant put him in charge of the Army of the Shenandoah with orders to clear all Confederate troops out of the

Shenandoah Valley. Sheridan defeated Jubal Early's Confederate forces in several battles, capturing five thousand of his men. He cleared the Shenandoah Valley and then destroyed much of the property and supplies there. Although this destruction bothered Sheridan, he knew it was necessary that this valley—long used as a pathway of invasion—be stripped of resources so that it could no longer support the Confederate Army marching north. For his success in the valley, he received special recognition from Congress.

★ SHERMAN, WILLIAM TECUMSEH (1820–1891)

Known for his historic, devastating "March to the Sea," William Tecumseh Sherman commanded a Union brigade at Bull Run (Manassas) in the earlier years of the war and later played important roles in the Battle of Shiloh and the Vicksburg campaign.

After taking control of Atlanta in 1864, the opinionated and self-assured Sherman convinced his superiors to allow him to march his troops through the heart of Georgia to split the Confederacy in two. Sherman insisted that "if we can march a well-appointed army right through [Jefferson Davis's] territory, it is a demonstration to the world, foreign and domestic, that we have a power which Davis cannot resist." Sherman and his troops spread out to a distance of twenty-five to sixty miles and destroyed virtually everything that might have had military value to the Confederates, including farms, plantations, and railroads. They found adequate food along the way, destroying what they didn't eat. Sherman believed in total war, that the Union armies had to destroy the ability of the South to sustain the war, not just defeat its armies in battle. "We are not only fighting hostile enemies, but a hostile people," Sherman said, "and must make old and young, rich and poor, feel the hard hand of war." In December 1864, Sherman sent a wire to President Lincoln saying, "I beg to present you, as a Christmas gift, the city of Savannah."

After the war, supporters urged Sherman to run for president, but he steadfastly refused to enter politics.

★ SHILOH, BATTLE OF (PITTSBURG LANDING)

An intense two-day battle near Pittsburg Landing, Tennessee, was named for the little white church—"Shiloh"—around which the fighting raged. On the morning of April 6, 1862, Confederate General Albert Sidney Johnston led the attack on General Ulysses S. Grant's Union troops. The South pushed the northern troops back, but Johnston was killed. His command was taken by General P.G.T. Beauregard, who shortly thereafter wired Confederate President Jefferson Davis that he had won a "complete" victory. He had not. The Union troops under Grant would not retreat. During the rain-soaked night, reinforcements arrived. The next day, the Union force attacked Beauregard's thirty thousand weary men with nearly twice that number, forcing them to withdraw.

The northern troops had assumed that they would unite at Shiloh and then plunge farther south into Mississippi. The combined armies of Grant and General Don Carlos Buell had beaten back the Confederates but at a cost of too many dead. They were not in a position to march through the South and end the war as quickly as they had hoped. Of the one hundred thousand Union and Confederate men who fought at Shiloh, nearly one-quarter—twenty-five thousand—were killed, wounded, captured, or missing.

★ SICKLES, DANIEL (1819–1914)

Daniel Sickles, a Union corps commander during the war, had a reputation as a womanizer and a heavy drinker. His troops had a reputation as some of the most rowdy in the army. However, Sickles was respected for his courage and distinguished himself at the Seven Days' and Fredericksburg battles.

At Gettysburg, the always controversial Sickles was displeased with the Cemetery Ridge area he had been assigned to defend. He disobeyed orders and moved his troops to lower ground in a peach orchard and in doing so was trapped between Union and Confederate lines. James Longstreet's Confederate troops bombarded Sickles's men with artillery, but they were still able to retreat to Union lines. Sickles then led his men and fresh troops on attacks through the Wheat Field, Devil's Den, and the Valley of Death, all places where it was said that bullets whizzed by so fast and thick that you could wave a hat in the air and fill it with lead. Sickles had his leg nearly blown off during the battle. But when he was carried from the field, with his shredded leg dangling from his body, he was not only conscious, but was smoking a cigar and talking to his men. He later donated his amputated leg to a medical museum, visiting the museum after the war to see his leg on display!

★ SMALLS, ROBERT (1839–1915)

Thousands of slaves escaped to the North during the war, but few in as dramatic fashion as Robert Smalls. He was the pilot of a Confederate supply ship, and one night in 1862 when the captain was ashore in Charleston, Smalls and a group of men stole the ship. Smalls guided it out of Charleston harbor, and then turned the vessel over to Union ships blockading the harbor. He was rewarded not only with his freedom, but also with a job in the Union Navy as a warship pilot. After the war, he returned to his home in Beaufort, South Carolina, and became an advocate for African-American rights. He was elected to the state constitutional convention and fought

Robert Smalls

for the right of blacks to receive free public education equal to that provided to whites.

★ SPOTSYLVANIA COURT HOUSE, BATTLE OF

The Battle of Spotsylvania Court House is one of four major battle sites near Fredericksburg, Virginia (Fredericksburg, Chancellorsville, and the Wilderness are the other three). The combined 110,000 casualties in that area are said to make it the bloodiest ground in North America. In May 1864, Confederate General Robert E. Lee won an important victory over Ulysses Grant's troops at Spotsylvania. The battle began the day after the Battle of the Wilderness ended. At Spotsylvania, Grant combined his army into three corps, bringing his total manpower to 118,000, while Lee's troops numbered only 63,000. The South suffered more than 9,000 casualties at Spotsylvania, the North more than twice as many. The hand-to-hand

A Confederate soldier, one of the nine thousand casualties at Spotsylvania, lies dead after the battle. Photographers generally posed the bodies after they were dead. This soldier was probably propped against the breastworks (wooden barricades used to shield the soldier as he fired his rifle), with the rifle leaned against him.

combat at Spotsylvania, much of it in the pouring rain, was fierce. "I never expect to be fully believed when I tell what I saw of the horrors of Spotsylvania," wrote a Union officer, "because I should be loath to believe it myself were the case reversed." The northern press reported that Grant appeared headed for Richmond and an end to the war. But he couldn't break through Lee's lines. The optimism in the North quickly faded, at least temporarily. For the South, the price of victory was high. Lee lost more than one-third of his commanders. It was difficult enough for the South to replace soldiers but finding new commanding officers was nearly impossible. Lee's Army of Northern Virginia never fully regained its former fighting capability after Spotsylvania.

⭐ STANTON, EDWIN McMASTERS (1814–1869)

After Lincoln's first secretary of war, Simon Cameron, resigned in 1862 because of accusations of corruption, Lincoln appointed Edwin Stanton to the position. A former lawyer and the attorney general during Buchanan's presidency, Stanton was strongly opposed to slavery. He disagreed with many of Lincoln's policies, and alienated government officials with his efficient and honest, but harsh, manner.

Stanton was thought of as stubborn, arrogant, and often unjust, but he was successful in ridding the war department of the waste and fraud allowed by his predecessors. The resulting "housecleaning" by Stanton, meant more money to provide troops with badly needed weapons and supplies.

⭐ STATES' RIGHTS

Slavery has always been considered the major cause of the Civil War. However, a more complicated constitutional issue, which dated back to the Revolutionary War, was at the center of the controversy between North and South. The issue of states' rights—what power, or rights, the states hold, and what power is held by the federal government—as much as slavery split the nation.

The Constitution gives the states the right to enact laws not enacted by or already reserved for the federal government. Certainly slavery was a major economic issue to the South as much as an emotional issue to abolitionists. Without slave labor, Southerners feared their entire way of life and plantation economy would crumble. But the free states argued that slavery was an issue to be decided at the federal level, not by individual states. The constitutional interpretation in the Dred Scott case put the U.S. Supreme Court—and thus the U.S. government—indirectly in support of the South. If the South and slave states would not be allowed to determine their own destiny, the only solution was secession, according to southern leaders.

★ STEVENS, THADDEUS (1792–1868)

Thaddeus Stevens, a Pennsylvania lawyer and politician, was nearly seventy years old when the war began. He was known for promoting the belief in the equality of all men—rich or poor, black or white. By the time Lincoln was elected president in 1860, the strong antislavery movement in Congress had gained momentum. Stevens, elected to Congress in 1848, became part of a vocal group of antislavery legislators urging Lincoln to take harsher actions against the South. One of the strongest radical voices in Congress, Stevens wanted to "free every slave, slay every traitor." He rose to become chairman of the Ways and Means Committee in the House of Representatives, a position he used to help push numerous antislavery bills through Congress. Although Robert E. Lee forbade pil-

Thaddeus Stevens

laging private property in the North, not all southern troops obeyed. Confederates retaliated against Stevens for his antislavery efforts by destroying one of his businesses near Chambersburg, Pennsylvania. After the war and Lincoln's death, Stevens remained a vocal opponent of Lincoln's moderate reconstruction policies, calling for the South to be treated as a defeated country, not as states to be welcomed back into the Union.

★ STOWE, HARRIET BEECHER (1811–1896)

Harriet Beecher Stowe, a writer from a prominent New England family of preachers and educators, was perhaps the most significant author of the Civil War. In 1851, her novel *Uncle Tom's Cabin* (subtitled *Life Among the Lowly*) was first published in serial form in an abolitionist paper, *The National Era,* in Washington, DC. An indictment of slavery and its cruelty, *Uncle Tom's Cabin,* was read from North to South, and became the rallying point for the "Underground Railroad," the system of secret routes and hiding spots created by abolitionists to smuggle runaway slaves to freedom in the North. *Uncle Tom's Cabin* was published in book form in 1852 and sold an astounding three hundred thousand copies during that year. Stowe once said that it was the death of an infant son to cholera that moved her to action and empathy for the suffering of slave mothers.

Harriet Beecher Stowe

★ STUART, JAMES EWELL BROWN (J.E.B.) (1833–1864)

James Stuart, known as "Jeb," was twenty-eight years old when the war began. He quickly resigned from the U.S. Army to join the Confederacy in his home state of Virginia. One of the most famous cavalryman of the Civil War, Stuart was gallant, well liked, and quickly rose to the rank of general. He won distinction leading cavalry at the first and second battles of Bull Run, the Seven Days' Battles, and the battles of Antietam (Sharpsburg), Fredericksburg, Chancellorsville, Gettysburg, and the Wilderness. Stuart was also a raider, whom Robert E. Lee called "the eyes and ears of my army" for his value in obtaining information about the Union Army. In a recommendation for a promotion, General J. E. Johnston described Stuart as "calm, firm, acute, active and enterprising." General Early said that it was Stuart who "did as much toward saving the Battle of First Bull Run [Manassas]" as anyone. Jeb Stuart was killed in the Battle of the Wilderness at Yellow Tavern by Philip Sheridan's cavalry in 1864.

★ SURRATT, MARY E. (1820–1865)

There always has been some doubt about whether or not Mary Surratt was an active conspirator in the assassination of Lincoln. Nevertheless, she was hanged for the crime. The North was brimming with anger over the assassination of the president, and many were anxious to see all the alleged conspirators pay for the crime. Besides identifying the obvious assassin, John Wilkes Booth, a hasty trial did little to untangle the conspiracy and determine clearly the role of each of those on trial.

Surratt's son, John, had conspired with Booth months earlier to kidnap Lincoln, but the attempt never took place. Booth, John Surratt, and others often met in Mary Surratt's boardinghouse on H Street in downtown Washington. The

military trial that followed the killing of Booth—by soldiers tracking him after the shooting—was clearly anything but fair. Mary Surratt believed she would be convicted in the country's lust for someone to blame, but she never thought she would be executed. In all, four "conspirators" were hanged, including Surratt. Her son, John, was never caught and tried, having escaped to Canada.

Church bells tolled as thousands of people lined the streets of Washington, DC, to view the slow, grim spectacle of Lincoln's funeral parade. The president's body was carried to the Capitol, where it lay in state the next day.

★ TANEY, ROGER B. (1777–1864)

U.S. Supreme Court justices interpret laws that govern the entire country. Their appointment to the high court is for life. Supreme Court Chief Justice Robert B. Taney was eighty years old in 1857 when he made one of the most surprising and controversial rulings in the history of the U.S. Supreme Court. Dred Scott, a slave, sued for his freedom after his owner died. Taney said that slaves and their descendants could never have the right to sue in court because all blacks—slave or free—were not citizens according to the Constitution. Taney, ruling against Scott, also held that slaves did not become free just because they traveled to a free state. He went on to say that the Constitution gave Congress no authority to ban slavery in the territories, either. Taney's decision so endorsed the extension of slavery that it spurred Lincoln to run for the Senate against Stephen Douglas in 1858, a bid he lost before winning the presidency two years later. See *Dred Scott.*

★ THIRTEENTH AMENDMENT

Lincoln's Emancipation Proclamation is famous today for freeing slaves, but it did not free all the slaves. The proclamation abolished slavery in states in rebellion against the

Union, but the question remained of what would happen in those states after the war. Lincoln felt that a constitutional amendment was the only way to ensure that slavery would be ended in *all* of the United States forever. The House of Representatives and the Senate voted to end slavery, and once the amendment was ratified by the

THE THREE COSTLIEST BATTLES OF THE CIVIL WAR

The three battles with the most casualties (killed, wounded, missing, or captured on both sides) in the Civil War all took place in a nearly five-month period in 1863, the middle of the four years of conflict:

Union troops recuperate outside a makeshift hospital in Virginia during the war.

Gettysburg, July 1–3, 1863

As Robert E. Lee drove his Confederate troops into the North, the Union won at Gettysburg, the decisive battle that took the advantage and momentum away from the South and was critical to the outcome of the war. More than 150,000 troops met in the fierce battle and a full one-third were casualties—more than 50,000 all told in the three days of intense fighting.

Chickamauga, Georgia, September 19–20, 1863

William S. Rosecrans led 58,000 U.S. troops against the Confederate commander Braxton Bragg's 66,000 men. Bragg, with a rare southern manpower advantage, was victorious, despite suffering more than 18,000 casualties, 2,000 more than suffered by the Union.

Chancellorsville, Virginia, May 1–4, 1863

Robert E. Lee's army suffered 13,000 casualties (compared with Joseph Hooker's 17,000 for the North) in the battle in which Stonewall Jackson was wounded, dying shortly after. The North entered the battle with more than twice as many troops as the South at Chancellorsville (134,000 compared with the South's 60,000), but it was a major victory for the Confederacy, just two months before the South lost not only its momentum but a huge number of its commanders at Gettysburg.

states, it became law. The first ten Amendments to the Constitution—the Bill of Rights—were enacted in 1791. Amendments eleven and twelve followed in 1795 and 1804. It was sixty-one years later, in 1865, when the next amendment became law and slavery was abolished. See *Emancipation Proclamation*.

★ TRUTH, SOJOURNER (1797(?)–1883)

Sojourner Truth

Sojourner Truth was born in Hurley, New York, as a slave named Isabella Baumfree and had many different masters as a child. One of thirteen children, she never knew her siblings because they were quickly sold as slaves. In her teens, she was sold to John J. Dumont, who forced her to marry another of his slaves. She and her husband, Thomas, had five children, some of whom were also sold into slavery. In 1827, she escaped from Dumont and was taken in by a Quaker family who helped her get one of her children back. She was freed in 1827 when slavery was abolished in New York State. In 1843, she changed her name to Sojourner Truth, her self-proclaimed mission to travel and speak the truth of God's word, she said. Although she could neither read nor write, Truth spoke eloquently and forcefully to her audiences in support of women's rights and the abolition of slavery. During the Civil War, she sang and preached to make money for black Union soldiers, and after the war, she worked to persuade Congress to give land to former slaves. She gave her famous "Ain't I a Woman?" speech at the 1851 Women's Rights Convention in Akron, Ohio, which became a classic expression of women's rights.

★ TUBMAN, HARRIET (CA. 1821–1913)

Born on a Maryland plantation, Harriet Tubman suffered a fractured skull at the age of thirteen while defending another slave from a brutal master. Quick-thinking and strong-willed, she escaped from slavery in 1849 and settled in the North. One of the greatest "conductors" on the Underground Railroad, she gained the nickname "Moses" for her nearly twenty trips leading escaped slaves from the South to freedom in the "promised land" of the North and Canada. On one of her final trips before the Civil War began, Tubman traveled back to the plantation where she was born to guide her parents to freedom. During the war, Tubman offered her valuable, courageous services as a nurse and scout to Union forces in South Carolina. On at least one occasion, forty-year-old Tubman disguised herself as an old plantation slave so she could spy on Confederate troops. She was so despised and feared in the South that at one time a bounty of forty thousand dollars was offered for her capture, a huge sum in those days. After the war, she worked to expand the rights of black men and women, and operated a home for elderly blacks in Auburn, New York, where she lived with her parents.

Harriet Tubman

★ TURNER, NAT (1800–1831)

Long before the Civil War, southern hatred and fear of slaves—or worse, free black men—was inflamed in part by a man named Nat Turner, a Virginia slave. In 1831, Turner led seventy slaves on a brutal rampage, killing fifty-seven white farmers. Turner was captured two months later and hanged. After Turner's revolt, a great many Southerners were terrified and the vocal pro-slavery leaders pointed to this revolt as "proof" that blacks belong as slaves.

U

★ UNCLE TOM'S CABIN

The most famous piece of Civil War–era literature, *Uncle Tom's Cabin,* was first published in an antislavery newspaper in 1851. A year later, this story of the brutal treatment of southern slaves was published in book form and sold an astounding three hundred thousand copies within a year. The author, Harriet Beecher Stowe, was a forty-year-old

Stowe's book was not only a tremendous success in sales, it also had a profound impact on the abolitionist movement and generations to come.

Maine writer and the daughter, sister, and wife of abolitionist clergymen. She wrote the tale of Uncle Tom at night by candlelight, after putting her children to bed. Provoked by the Fugitive Slave Law to "make this whole nation feel what an accursed thing slavery is," as her sister put it, Stowe wrote the novel about the terrible hardships of southern slaves. She told of the suffering that slaves endured, being beaten by their masters, hunted down by dogs, and separated permanently from their families at slave auctions. Abolitionists quickly adopted the book as the symbol of their efforts to end slavery, while pro-slavery advocates saw it as no more than an insult to the southern way of life.

135,000 SETS, 270,000 VOLUMES SOLD.

UNCLE TOM'S CABIN

FOR SALE HERE.

AN EDITION FOR THE MILLION, COMPLETE IN 1 Vol., PRICE 37 1-2 CENTS.
" " IN GERMAN, IN 1 Vol, PRICE 50 CENTS.
" " IN 2 Vols., CLOTH, 6 PLATES, PRICE $1.50.
SUPERB ILLUSTRATED EDITION, IN 1 Vol, WITH 153 ENGRAVINGS,
PRICES FROM $2.50 TO $5.00.

The Greatest Book of the Age.

★ UNIFORMS

Contrary to popular belief, the Civil War was not all blue and gray. Many regiments had matched uniforms made by local seamstresses or assembled by local recruiters, and these outfits bore little resemblance to standard military-issue uniforms. The South was actually known for its "butternut" cotton clothes, which were light yellow or beige rather than gray, having been dyed with walnut oil.

Troops throughout the war found replacement clothing (from shoes and socks to shirts and jackets) almost nonexistent, so innovation was the key to staying dry and warm. Troops commonly took shoes, clothing, and other gear from battlefield casualties on either side to use in place of their own worn-out uniforms.

Soldiers most often had their photos taken as they left for training or were about to head into battle. They would pose with clean uniforms, an extra weapon or two, and any embellishments they could find. It was the best they would look for years.

★ U.S. SANITARY COMMISSION

Established in 1861, the U.S. Sanitary Commission was a volunteer organization that supplemented the government's programs and provided health information, medical sup-

The Sanitary Commission sent men and women to establish field offices in many locations, this one in Alexandria, Virginia.

plies, and care for wounded soldiers. The Commission collected donations of such items as food, socks, shirts, trousers, and bandages. Many people enclosed notes with their donations, wishing soldiers well or asking them to write back. Commission volunteers collected and sorted the donations and then mailed them to supply stations throughout the North, where they were distributed to Union soldiers.

A sample of some of the goods the Sanitary Commission in Washington, DC, supplied to troops and hospitals during a three-week period in May and June 1865:

Combs	84,436
Stretchers	22
Spoons	1,710
Soap (pounds)	312
Towels	56,625
Tin Cups	3,180
Tin Plates	3,050
Drawers (underwear)	24,261
Handkerchiefs	62,684
Suspenders (pairs)	29,684
Shirts, cotton	8,600
Shirts, woolen	25,354
Butter (pounds)	498
Chocolate (pounds)	993
Condensed Milk (pounds)	13,169
Sugar (pounds)	2,626
Tobacco, chewing (pounds)	14,632
Tobacco, smoking (pounds)	6,016
Tomatoes (cans)	34,646
Crutches (pairs)	108
Canes	313
Envelopes	396,305
Ink (bottles)	4,855
Writing paper (sheets)	453,250
Pens	93,384
Pencils	15,558

The sanitary fairs in the North were not just successful; they were overwhelmingly so. This is the main building—of many—at the second fair held in Chicago.

The Sanitary Commission also sponsored fairs to raise money for additional medical equipment and other supplies. These so-called "sanitary fairs" were held in huge halls, where everything from baked goods to farm equipment was sold to raise money.

President Lincoln helped raise money at the Chicago Fair, donating his original manuscript for the Emancipation Proclamation. "I had some desire to retain the paper," Lincoln said, "but if it shall contribute to the relief and comfort of the soldiers, that will be better." It was purchased for the then-incredible sum of $3,000 by T. R. Bryan, President of the Chicago Soldiers' Home.

This is an actual copy of a congressional directory, signed "A. Lincoln." Lincoln signed his name A. Lincoln far more often than his full name. While not sold at a sanitary fair, this autographed copy was in the Gideon Welles family from the Civil War until sold more than 125 years later.

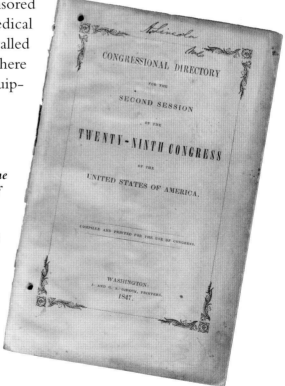

★ VICKSBURG, BATTLE OF, MISSISSIPPI

"Vicksburg is the key to winning the war," Lincoln said. In his youth, Lincoln had spent several years on the Mississippi and knew the value of the river to the survival of the South. Vicksburg was critical to keeping the southern army supplied. Grant and his army spent more than two months battling the swamps around the city in an attempt to seize strategic bluffs nearby.

Grant tried sending Sherman to tear up railroad tracks as a diversion and to carry out assaults through the bayous. But he could not break through Confederate defenses. Finally, after marching down the western banks of the Mississippi, he took Jackson (the capital of Mississippi) and continually hammered at Vicksburg with artillery fire.

Grant's men had marched nearly two hundred miles, fought and won five battles along the way, and then surrounded Vicksburg, trapping more than thirty thousand Confederate troops in the city. But he couldn't capture the town, so he was determined to lay siege to it, battering it with cannon fire until its only choice was to surrender.

Jefferson Davis called Robert E. Lee to Richmond with a plea for him to stop Grant. Instead, while Grant was outside Vicksburg, Lee marched his men north into southern Pennsylvania, hoping to force Grant to abandon Vicksburg and return to defend Washington. In July 1863, Lee's plans ended with defeat at Gettysburg, and Confederate troops at Vicksburg finally exhausted food supplies and were forced to surrender the city.

On May 23 and 24, 1865, two hundred thousand Union soldiers marched in a "grand review" along Pennsylvania Avenue in Washington, DC. Civilians and solemn disabled veterans lined the streets along the parade route. In the South, Confederate soldiers were heroes, too, but for most, their receptions were less glorious. Most were greeted by homes, plantations, and families in shambles.

★ WELLES, GIDEON (1802–1878)

During the Civil War, Secretary of the Navy Gideon Welles was a man Lincoln praised for his hard work and creativity. Welles had been a newspaperman and Democrat before the war. He switched to the new Republican party over the issue of slavery. Welles took a makeshift, peacetime fleet of forty-one vessels and turned it into a strong naval force of more than four hundred ships.

★ WHIG PARTY

For almost thirty years the Whig party was one of the two leading political parties in the United States. Abraham Lincoln served in Congress as a Whig. The key points differentiating the two major parties were long-simmering arguments over where political power should lie. The Whigs believed in a strong central government, with the federal government controlling national policy. The Democrats believed in a stronger voice for the individual states. Support for the Whig party declined rapidly, primarily because of the issue of slavery. The Compromise of 1850, which probably postponed the Civil War, was a result of the political genius of Whig Henry Clay. But it alienated many northern party members, and the Whigs began to become fragmented. Southern Whigs, in turn, looked to other candidates when the party nominated Winfield Scott for president in 1852. The new Republican party began to formulate its own platform based on a strong central government, and the Whigs soon disappeared altogether. Longtime Whig Lincoln was the new Republican party's first presidential candidate in 1860, adding freshness and an unwavering sense of constitutional government to the political picture.

★ WHITMAN, WALT (1819–1892)

More than 150 years after his first poems were published, Walt Whitman is still one of the world's most well-known poets. Whitman self-published his first poetry collection, *Leaves of Grass,* in 1855 after he was unable to find a publisher who would accept it. But he was gaining notoriety for his writing by the time the Civil War began. Whitman went to Washington, DC, in 1862 to care for a brother who was wounded at Fredericksburg. He stayed there the rest of the war, working as a nurse aiding recuperating Union soldiers injured in battle. These experiences led him to write a series of poems about the war titled *Drum-Taps,* while Lincoln's death moved him to create "O Captain, My Captain," one of the poems read by students in the United States for more than a century.

★ WILDERNESS, BATTLE OF THE

One of the great battles of the Civil War, Grant and Lee's meeting in May 1864 was in an entangled, overgrown area in Virginia known simply as the Wilderness. The area was dense with "thorny underbrush, and twisted vines . . . an almost

AN ARMY CORPS ON THE MARCH

With its cloud of skirmishers in advance,
With now the sound of a single shot, snapping like a whip, and now an irregular volley,
The swarming ranks press on and on, the dense brigades press on;
Glittering dimly, toiling under the sun—the dust-cover'd men,
In columns rise and fall to the undulations of the ground,
With artillery interspers'd—the wheels rumble, the horses sweat,
As the army *corps* advances.
—*Walt Whitman*

impassable labyrinth . . . reached only by unused and overgrown farm roads." Grant was marching his troops south and was less than twenty miles west of Fredericksburg as he began his spring campaign. Lee's army was nearby, and despite the loss at Gettysburg, he was optimistic. Undermanned as usual, the Confederate troops had been alerted by lookouts that the Army of the Potomac was moving. Grant hoped to cut through Lee's men and put his army between the Army of Northern Virginia and the city of Richmond. Some experts feel that military strategist Lee chose the Wilderness in which to fight because the terrain camouflaged his lack of manpower. The two-day battle, which involved only ten hours of actual fighting, ended with neither side gaining a clear advantage. Still, with smoke as thick as the underbrush hiding both the troops firing and the soldiers fallen, the combined North and South wounded and killed was nearly thirty thousand—three thousand per hour! The standoff was a strategic victory for Lee, who inflicted twice the casualties on Grant than he suffered. Grant was slowed, casualties were high, but the Union commander pushed on. His exhausted men were harassed by Confederate snipers and troops who felled trees to slow them even more.

★ WIRZ, HENRY (1822–1865)

From March 1864 until the end of the war, Henry Wirz was the commandant at Andersonville, the notorious Confederate prison in Georgia. After the war, Wirz was tried and found guilty of war crimes—failing to treat prisoners humanely—because of the prison's complete disregard for the health and survival of its prisoners. He claimed that he was only following Confederate government orders. Wirz was judged to be directly responsible for the deaths and suffering of thousands at Andersonville and was hanged in Washington, DC, on November 10, 1865.

★ ZOUAVES

The Zouave regiments were so named because of their distinctive uniforms modeled after French military styles. The often brilliantly colored uniforms—consisting of baggy pants with a sash at the waist, white canvas leggings, short vest and jacket, and a tasseled hat—were considered foreign and exotic and brought attention to any unit wearing them. While best known as northern troops, there were Zouave regiments on both sides during the Civil War.

The origins of the Zouaves can be traced to the Zouaoua, a fierce Arab tribe living in the rocky hills of Algeria and Morocco. In the 1830s, some of the Zouaoua joined the French colonial army as two auxiliary battalions. They quickly proved their worth in battle and became known for

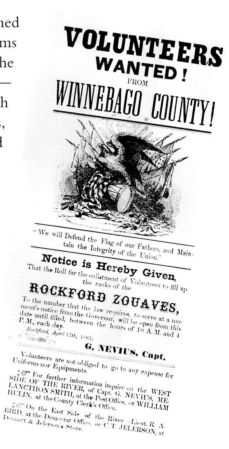

their smooth skirmish tactics and skillful use of bayonets. The "Zouave" units—as they were called by the French—were increasingly composed of native Frenchmen, but they continued to wear the distinctive uniforms of the North African Zouaoua. During an overseas mission, army Captain George B. McClellan observed the Zouaves and described them as "the finest light infantry that Europe can produce." It was not long before some American militia units adopted the Zouave style of uniforms.

Glossary

Battery   A group of guns typically placed along a fort wall or on the battlefield. A battle might have numerous batteries in strategic places on the battlefield, or a fort might have a dozen different battery placements to protect against attack.

Battles, Names of   Confusion often exists regarding which Civil War battle is which; this is because the North and South often had different names for battles. For example, when first studying Civil War history, adults as well as students often discuss Manassas and Bull Run as if they're different places! We have used the commonly accepted names for major battles where North and South identify battles differently, Bull Run (Manassas), Antietam (Sharpsburg), and Shiloh (Pittsburg Landing). Bull Run and Antietam are the Union names, while Shiloh is the Confederate name. The Confederates typically named battles after a nearby town, while the Union named battles for landmarks such as rivers or streams.

Bite the Bullet   The expression which has come to mean "toughen up" and bear the pain was a literal statement during the Civil War. Soldiers were given bullets, the same as the ones used on the battlefields, to bite down on to help them combat the lack of anesthetic, even during a battlefield amputation.

★ *October 1859*
John Brown attacks Harpers Ferry

★ *November 6, 1860*
Abraham Lincoln elected president

★ *December 20, 1860*
South Carolina secedes from the Union

★ *February 9, 1861*
Confederate States of America officially formed; Jefferson Davis elected president

★ *March 4, 1861*
Abraham Lincoln sworn in as sixteenth President of the United States

★ *April 12, 1861*
Confederates attack Fort Sumter; the Civil War begins

★ *July 21, 1861*
Battle of Bull Run

Blockade (Naval) Ships positioned close enough together along a coastline or near a port to prevent other ships from coming or going. The North successfully blockaded southern shipping during much of the war, preventing foreign countries from delivering much-needed supplies to the South and preventing the South from exporting cotton.

Broadside A printed sheet, such as a small poster, handed out or tacked up to advertise a meeting, promote candidates running for office, or announcing slave sales or arrivals of ships.

Casualty A soldier "lost" but not necessarily killed. Casualties included those missing in action, wounded, taken prisoner, or killed.

Debate Not just an argument but a structured presentation where opposing sides offer their views, comment on the opposition's views, and then respond. In the series of debates between Lincoln and Douglas in 1858, the comments and responses resulted in hundreds of pages published in book form before the Civil War.

Dysentery Very painful intestinal illness, accompanied by severe diarrhea. Virtually all prisoners suffered from it in prisoner-of-war camps, as did most troops throughout the North and South. It often caused death.

Freedmen's Bureau Agency formed near the end of the war to help former slaves find work, housing, and other necessities in the North.

"Great Emancipator" A name given to Lincoln by antislavery Northerners.

Impeachment This process, which was undertaken against Andrew Johnson (and President Bill Clinton 130 years later), is often misunderstood. Impeachment itself is the *process* by which Congress can bring charges against the president. If the president is found not guilty, as happened with both Johnson and Clinton, they indeed were impeached, but found innocent and continued to serve the remainder of their terms in office.

Indian "Wars"   U.S. soldiers continued fighting after the Civil War, waging wars against many different Indian "nations." Epitomizing the connection from decade to decade was George Armstrong Custer, who accepted the surrender flag at Appomattox, then led his men into complete annihilation by Indian warriors a decade later in Montana.

Kepi   The cap worn by Civil War soldiers that had a brim and somewhat resembled a modern baseball cap in size and shape.

"Little Giant"   Nickname of Stephen Douglas, senator and unsuccessful presidential candidate in 1860, who was quite short . . . but quite a powerful speaker.

Mexican War   The United States fought a war with Mexico from 1846–1848 and won territory that now is California, Nevada, Arizona, New Mexico, and Utah. Nearly fifteen thousand U.S. soldiers were killed, and many of the Civil War's military leaders—North and South—fought side by side against Mexico.

Ordnance   Military weapons, ammunition, and supplies.

Our American Cousin   The play that was being performed at Ford's Theatre in Washington, DC, the night Lincoln was shot.

Picket   Soldier at the edge of camp standing guard to warn if any enemy troops were approaching.

★ *July 4, 1863*
Vicksburg surrendered

★ *September 19–20, 1863*
Battle of Chickamauga

★ *November 19, 1863*
Lincoln delivers the Gettysburg Address

★ *May 5–6, 1864*
Battle of the Wilderness

★ *May 8–12, 1864*
Battle of Spotsylvania

★ *June 1–3, 1864*
Battle of Cold Harbor

★ *June 15, 1864*
A nine-month siege of Petersburg begins

★ *September 2, 1864*
Atlanta captured by Sherman's army

★ *November 8, 1864*
Abraham Lincoln re-elected president

★ *December 21, 1864*
Sherman captures Savannah, Georgia, after his destructive 300-mile long, 60-mile wide "March to the Sea"

☆ *January 31, 1865*
U.S. Congress approves
Thirteenth Amendment
to the Constitution,
abolishing slavery.

☆ *February 3, 1865*
Hampton Roads Peace
Conference

☆ *March 25, 1865*
The last offensive for
Lee's Army of Northern
Virginia begins with an
attack on the center of
Grant's forces at
Petersburg. Four hours
later the attack is broken.

☆ *April 2, 1865*
Richmond, the
Confederate capital, is
evacuated.

☆ *April 9, 1865*
Lee surrenders his army
to Grant at Appomattox

☆ *April 14, 1865*
President Lincoln is shot

☆ *April 15, 1865*
President Abraham
Lincoln dies at 7:22 in
the morning.

☆ *May 1865*
Remaining Confederate
forces surrender. The
nation is reunited as the
Civil War ends.

Platform (Political)   The list of views and specific programs supported by a candidate or group (ticket/party) of candidates. In the Civil War this might have included supporting antislavery legislation, proposing new economic acts to strengthen either North or South, supporting stronger state government/rights rather than those of the federal government, and so on.

Regiment   A standard fighting group of soldiers (also referred to as a "unit"), typically one thousand, but the size varied during the Civil War. Regiments were formed in and around communities, and as the war dragged on, recruits seldom kept pace with casualties. The result was much smaller but experienced regiments being rebuilt with new recruits, or depleted regiments being combined to form one new regiment.

Sanitary Fair   These fairs held in the North to raise money for medical and other supplies for the Union Army were much more than a typical county fair of the nineteenth century. Huge halls were built to display, auction, and sell tens of thousands of items. The massive central buildings were often larger than modern airplane hangars.

Sherman's Neckties   The name Union troops gave to the torn-up and bent rails that Sherman's army left in its wake as they marched through the South, destroying most everything in their path.

Ticket (Political)   A ticket is the group of candidates representing the same political party or just representing the same views—Lincoln-Johnson and possibly a senator and congressman would form the "Republican" ticket in Illinois.

Tintype   A small image (3x3 or 4x4 inches) that was processed on metal, not paper or cardboard. Often tintypes were encased in an ornate frame, many of which were lined with velvet and could be clasped shut.

Torpedoes   David Farragut was famous for "damning" them, and in the Civil War they were floating mines that exploded and damaged or sunk a ship. Modern submarines fire cigar-shaped torpedoes that race under the water's surface like car-length motorized bombs while Civil War torpedoes were floating or tethered metal "basketballs" that exploded when bumped by a ship.

December 6, 1865
The Thirteenth Amendment to the United States Constitution, passed by Congress on January 31, 1865, is ratified. Slavery is abolished.

Selected Reading and Notes on the Research

There have been tens of thousands of books written about the Civil War. They were published during and immediately after the war, and there is no sign of slowing 140 years later. Some are good; some are horrid. Often, one cannot tell what is accurate and what is fantasy. Many Civil War veterans wrote down their stories in the late nineteenth century. Separating fact from suspect recollections can be difficult. Read the best writers, the best historians first. James M. McPherson provides the best foundation, with sound history and fine writing. Study the newspapers of any city in the United States from the 1850s until the end of the war. They tell us what was on the minds of those fighting the war, directing the battles, and waiting for their loved ones to return. And they are remarkably accessible in libraries throughout the country.

Researching a topic so vast as the War Between the States is daunting for any writer—a middle-aged author of many books and a middle-school student faced with the need to present a thousand words on Lincoln or Grant by Monday morning.

Libraries will always be the key to history, but the Internet has opened countless new doors. Historical societies, for example, in communities as small as a few hundred people, now have Web sites with fabulous information previously difficult to find.

Many of the books listed below tell dramatic stories in addition to the history they report. Many authors had a particular interest or reason for writing a book. For example, Chittenden's book includes the note that it "has grown out of my love and respect for Abraham Lincoln; knowing no way in which I can better attest the sincerity of its purpose I dedicate it to his son, Robert T. Lincoln, minister of the United States to the Court of St. James." Wright's book states simply that it was written "in loving memory of two Confederate Soldiers, my father and my brother."

Having developed this seven-book series on the Civil War, I'm aware that the immense research and writing about the subject shows no signs of slowing. Previously unknown facts, documents, and photographs are still being unearthed today and will be tomorrow, as well.

SELECTED BIBLIOGRAPHY OF BOOKS

Abbot, Willis J., *Battle Fields and Camp Fires: A Narrative of the Principal Military Operations of the Civil War.* (New York: Dodd, Mead & Company, 1890).

Anderson, J. Cutler., *The South Reports the Civil War.* (Princeton, NJ: Princeton University Press, 1970).

Anonymous. *Famous Adventures and Prison Escapes of the Civil War.* (New York: The Century Company, 1913).

Blackford, Charles Minor III, ed., *Letters from Lee's Army, or, Memoirs of Life in and Out of the Army in Virginia During the War Between the States.* (New York: Charles Scribner's Sons, 1947).

Burton, E. P., *Diary of E. P. Burton: Surgeon 7th Reg. Ill. 3rd Brig. 2nd Div. 16 A.C.* (Des Moines, IA: The Historical Records Survey, 1939).

Chittenden, L. E., *Recollection of President Lincoln and His Administration.* (New York: Harper & Brothers, 1891).

DeKay, James Tertius, *Monitor: The Story of the Legendary Civil War Ironclad and the Man Whose Invention Changed the Course of History.* (New York: Walker and Company, 1997).

Doubleday, Abner, *Reminiscences of Forts Sumter and Moultrie in 1860–61.* (Fort Sumter National Monument Library, 1876. Reprint. Spartanburg, SC: The Reprint Company, 1976).

Fleming, Walter Lynwood, *The Sequel of Appomattox: A Chronicle of the Reunion of the States.* (New Haven, CT: Yale University Press, 1919).

Freedman, Russell, *Lincoln: A Photobiography.* (New York: Clarion Books, 1987).

Gross, Warren Lee, *The Soldier's Story of His Captivity at Andersonville, Belle Isle and Other Rebel Prisons.* (Boston: Lee & Shepard, 1866).

Hakim, Joy, *War, Terrible War.* (New York: Oxford University Press, 1994).

Hutton, Paul Andrew, ed., *The Custer Reader.* (Lincoln, NB: University of Nebraska Press, 1992).

Karolevitz, Robert F., *From Quill to Computer: The Story of America's Community Newspapers.* (National Newspaper Foundation, 1985).

Livermore, Mary A., *My Story of the War: A Woman's Narrative.* (Hartford, CT: A. D. Worthington & Company, 1889).

Logan, Mrs. John A., *Reminiscences of a Soldier's Wife.* (New York: Charles Scribner's Sons, 1913).

McPherson, James M., *Battle Cry of Freedom: The Civil War Era.* (New York: Ballantine Books, 1988).

Meltzer, Milton, *Voices from the Civil War.* (New York: Thomas Y. Crowell, 1989).

Morrow, Honore Willsie, *The Lost Speech of Abraham Lincoln.* (New York: Frederick A. Stokes Company, 1925).

Pfanz, Harry W., *Gettysburg: Culp's Hill & Cemetery Hill.* (Chapel Hill, NC: The University of North Carolina Press, 1993).

Photographic History of the Civil War, 10 vols.; reprint of the original 1911 50th anniversary of the war edition. (Secaucus, NJ: The Blue & Grey Press, 1987).

Political Debates Between Hon. Abraham Lincoln and Hon. Stephen A. Douglas, in the Celebrated Campaign of 1858, in Illinois. (Columbus, OH: Follett, Foster and Company, 1860).

Sifakis, Stewart, *Who Was Who in the Civil War.* (New York: Facts on File Publications, 1988).

Ward, Geoffrey C., *The Civil War: An Illustrated History.* (New York: Alfred A. Knopf, 1990).

Additional books developed and edited by Norman Bolotin and Christine Laing provide excellent material for young readers

studying the Civil War. Published by Dutton Children's Books and Puffin Books, they include:

A Nation Torn: The Story of How the Civil War Began and *Behind the Blue and Gray: The Soldier's Life in the Civil War,* by Delia Ray; *A Separate Battle: Women and the Civil War,* by Ina Chang; and *For Home and Country, A Civil War Scrapbook,* by Norman Bolotin and Angela Herb. They produced additional volumes for Dutton on the postwar Reconstruction era, as well as on the Klondike gold rush and the westward expansion of the post–Civil War United States.

Acknowledgments

This is the ninth book we have created for Penguin Putnam/Dutton Children's Books. I would be remiss not to thank former publisher, Christopher Franceschelli, long-time editorial director of the former Lodestar imprint, Virginia Buckley, and the persevering Donna Brooks, who has been forced to play the role of politician and psychologist as well as senior editor on this project. Rosanne Lauer demonstrated superb perspective and meticulous attention to detail in both copyediting and fact-checking.

Christine Laing, my partner, wife, and editorial director in our book development business since 1985 (first Laing Communications Inc. and now The History Bank) pretty much ensured the launch of this series and, on numerous occasions, the survival as well as editorial quality of the program.

Sandra Harner, with whom Chris and I have worked since 1974, is art director, book designer, emergency proofreader, photo retoucher, and anything else needed to ensure success. She creates good books despite the roadblocks so often placed in her way.

Laura Fisher, who left our company in early 2000 to work in the performing arts and add a new baby to her life, spent parts of three years on this book, researching, editing, and writing while simultaneously working on numerous other books with Chris, Sandi, and me. People with these skills and talents seldom receive the recognition they should.

Please look at the many archives listed in the photo credits. These, and many other libraries and museums and archives on the Internet, deserve our thanks. Putting together a book such as this requires help and cooperation from more people than most would guess.

Since we have worked on Civil War books for almost ten years, many of the same people have shared their kindnesses and expertise on one, two, or even all of the books. These include Brian Pohanka, one of the most knowledgeable Civil War historians in the country; Thomas J. McCarthy, a longtime friend and colleague, and a Civil War walking encyclopedia; Kean Wilcox, an immense help on Civil War photography; Leib Photo Archives, a resource for everyone and a key to the Library of Congress; and Andrea Telli, special collections archivist at the Chicago Public Library's Harold Washington Center, whose unflagging help has made our books better (and so much easier to produce) time and time again.

Illustration and Photo Credits

Many of the photographs listed here are available from a variety of sources. Those of us writing about and studying the Civil War are fortunate to have numerous public and private libraries, institutions, archives, and other sources for a broad photographic history of the war. In researching the Civil War since the late 1980s, we have compiled a substantial archive and database of photos, reference materials, and artifacts. The photos and illustrations included in this book have come from our own collection, from major institutions, and from smaller university and private collections.

The following references are intended to help with any additional research you may undertake. We have included references for one previous book in the Penguin Putnam/ Dutton *Young Readers' History of the Civil War*, as many of our materials have been used in the same or modified form in one or more of our previous books, as well as here. We have also included a reference, often one of several, where you may find the image.

One can never overstate the gratitude that we as researchers and writers have for the librarians and archivists who make books like this possible. A reference collection is only as valuable as its accessibility to everyone.

Front cover (upper left, top to bottom): *Behind the Blue and Gray*, Library of Congress; *For Home and Country*, Chicago Public Library, Special Collections Department; *A Nation Torn*, Library of Congress; *A Nation Torn*, Library of Congress; (upper right, top to bottom): *Behind the Blue and Gray*, Library of Congress; *Behind the Blue and Gray*, Library of Congress; *A Separate Battle*,

Moorland-Spingarn Research Center, Howard University; *Behind the Blue and Gray*, National Archives.

Back cover (upper left, top to bottom): *Till Victory Is Won*, Leib Image Archives; *A Nation Torn*, Library of Congress; *Till Victory Is Won*, Chicago Historical Society; *For Home and Country*, Collection of Kean Wilcox; (upper right, top to bottom): *Reconstruction*, Library of Congress; *For Home and Country*, Collection of Kean Wilcox; *Till Victory Is Won*, Library of Congress; *Reconstruction*, Chicago Historical Society

41   *Till Victory Is Won*, Leib Image Archives
42   Both photos: *Till Victory Is Won*, Moorland-Spingarn Research Center,
     Howard University
43   *A Nation Torn*, Library of Congress
45   *For Home and Country*, Norman Bolotin and Christine Laing, The History Bank
46   Norman Bolotin and Christine Laing, The History Bank
47   *A Nation Torn*, Library of Congress
49   *A Nation Torn*, Library of Congress
50   *Till Victory Is Won*, Library of Congress
51   *A Nation Torn*, Library of Congress
53   *Reconstruction*, Library of Congress
55   Top: *Behind the Blue and Gray*, U.S. Army Military History Institute
     Bottom: *A Nation Torn*, Library of Congress
57   *Behind the Blue and Gray*, Eleanor S. Brockenbrough Library, The Museum of
     the Confederacy
60   *Behind the Blue and Gray*, U.S. Army Military History Institute
61   *Reconstruction*, National Museum of American History, Smithsonian Institution
62   Norman Bolotin and Christine Laing, The History Bank
63   Top: *Behind the Blue and Gray*, National Archives
     Bottom: *A Nation Torn*, Library of Congress
65   *Behind the Blue and Gray*, National Archives
66   *A Nation Torn*, Library of Congress
67   Norman Bolotin and Christine Laing, The History Bank
69   *For Home and Country*, Chicago Public Library, Special Collections Department
70   *Reconstruction*, Leib Image Archives
71   *Reconstruction*, Library of Congress
72   *Behind the Blue and Gray*, Library of Congress
73   *A Nation Torn*, National Archives
74   *A Nation Torn*, Library of Congress
75   Both photos: *Behind the Blue and Gray*, Library of Congress
76   *A Nation Torn*, Library of Congress
78   Norman Bolotin and Christine Laing, The History Bank
80   *A Nation Torn*, Library of Congress
81   *A Separate Battle*, Library of Congress
82   Top: Norman Bolotin and Christine Laing, The History Bank
     Bottom: *For Home and Country*, Chicago Public Library, Special Collections
     Department
83   *For Home and Country*, Chicago Public Library, Special Collections Department
84   *For Home and Country*, Chicago Public Library, Special Collections Department
85   *For Home and Country*, Chicago Public Library, Special Collections Department
86   *Behind the Blue and Gray*, National Archives
87   *Behind the Blue and Gray*, Library of Congress
88   *For Home and Country*, Leib Image Archives
89   Norman Bolotin and Christine Laing, The History Bank
90   *Behind the Blue and Gray*, National Archives
91   Top: *A Separate Battle*, U.S. Army Military History Institute
     Bottom: *For Home and Country*, Chicago Public Library, Special Collections
     Department

MONTICELLO PUBLIC LIBRARY
512 E. LAKE AVE.
MONTICELLO, WI 53570